The Keeper

A Witness for the Demon Series

By Kevin Wollenweber

This book is a work of fiction. Any resemblance to actual events or persons, living or dead, is entirely coincidental.

"The Keeper," by Kevin Wollenweber. ISBN 978-1-63868-087-1 (softcover); 978-1-63868-088-8 (eBook).

Published 2022 by Virtualbookworm.com Publishing Inc., P.O. Box 9949, College Station, TX 77842, US. ©2022, Kevin Wollenweber. All rights reserved. No part of this publication may be reproduced, stored in a retrieval system, or transmitted in any form or by any means, electronic, mechanical, recording or otherwise, without the prior written permission of Kevin Wollenweber.

This novel is dedicated to
Nancy Jane.

A truly great writer and inspiration.

Preface

Chapter 55: Requiem / A Witness for the Demon

Staring at and taking in the drama that this drunk loser was displaying, the hooded figure that had been sitting next to him, all night as he drank himself to oblivion, made his move. Plotting and confirming that this was the right choice to try again, to get back in the game, he had made his decision.

Demetri entered this kid's mind and soul to prepare it for his master. This time he would not fail, he could not, and he would be restored.

THE "KEEPER" BEGINS with Demetri's resurrection and restoration by Lucifer, after his banishment to Hades by the Angel Gabriel, and prior to his return to Earth. It is my desire for you, the reader, to understand the sequence of events that lead to Demetri's return to once again harvest souls for *his* master. The second chapter will bring you up to speed on the blossoming relationship of Courtney and Alex and where that relationship stands just before the start of the third chapter. The third chapter begins precisely where the first book, "A Witness for the Demon", ended. Witness the power of evil at work and the struggles of those that battle against that evil. Enjoy.

Kevin Wollenweber

Chapter 1:
The Abyssal

HIS PAIN WAS TOO MUCH TO ENDURE. It had been over three thousand years since Demetri had felt these torturous sensations that were engulfing his entire being. The pain of a thousand needles piercing one's human flesh could not come close to what he was now experiencing. Blinded, he had no vision to see his surroundings, and the only sounds he could hear were the anguished cries of fellow demons and lost souls, much like the constant drone of a beehive now permeating his hearing. Those cries caused him to be afraid. He had never felt fear. Not at this place. Those feelings had been foreign to him before. Now, they would haunt him forever.

He had been a magnificent angel in Lucifer's legion and once had worshipped Gabriel's God with all the fervor and vigor of a serving Angel. Lucifer, before the time of the fall, directed and provided for Demetri as he had all those who were part of the heavenly host. He became to Demetri as powerful and beautiful as Gabriel's God they had once worshipped. His admiration of Lucifer was how he became attracted to his beauty and persuasiveness. Lucifer's spirit was so engaging that he made Demetri want to believe he was equal to Gabriel's God.

Because of his allegiance, Demetri was offered a choice to follow Lucifer or Gabriel's God. He believed Lucifer to be equal to the creator. This very decision caused him to be cast out of the only home he had known since his creation as an Angel. Cast away from that time of peace, tranquility, and love for his fellow Angels. Separated forever from his Heavenly home, cast to *this* existence, this abyss of pain and suffering with only his master Lucifer to depend upon to squelch the current torment he now felt, and the only way to defer this pain was to deliver the souls of earthly mortals to his master, Lucifer.

He had made his choice long ago and now must work to bring these mortal souls to the one he chose as *his* god.

Mortal souls provided the only buffer to the torment he now felt. Through them, Demetri had avoided the pain he must now experience and he knew that he must never question his master's dominion over these mortals of earth. For an angel of Satan to question Lucifer and deny his godliness would mean an eternity of what he now experienced. He had a job to do, and he was an efficient harvester for his master, until recently.

Demetri had committed the worst offense against his master that an angel could. He had failed at delivering a soul he had indwelled. There was nothing Lucifer despised more than losing a soul to Gabriel's God, and Demetri had done just that.

A soul that he still could not comprehend that he had lost. He writhed in pain as he remembered this loss. The young woman, Cindy Firestone was on the brink of being perhaps one of his greatest triumphs. She was a human that challenged him in every way, mortally and immortally. To dwell on her memory, was frankly, ungodly.

Had he been successful in the delivery of Cindy's soul, it would have brought him fame and favor with his fellow demons richer than he had ever known. Jealousy amongst the demons of Hades was normal. They always were an envious bunch. Now in this abyss, connected to the surface world by a single pathway that all who traveled to this underworld must, he was nothing more than a tormented creature. Void of any jealously and envy of any occupant soul.

From the very first time he was chosen by Lucifer to travel to the surface of earth, Demetri understood his mission. With that knowledge he had found favor with Lucifer. Not once had Demetri been sentenced to travel back down the Abyssal as a defeated angel. Until now.

Many demons rumored and he knew some believed that Gabriel's God was the one truly in control of the Abyssal Gateway. None of his fellow demons would openly suggest this to each other. To do so would be to question Lucifer's reign and power. He certainly would never question his master, except that through this current torment he lacked an understanding of why and how a mere mortal, Alex Dante, could see him, talk with him, and ultimately triumph over him? Why wasn't he told by Lucifer that mortals like Alex existed? Unless his master himself didn't know. He must have just been fortunate to never have encountered a mortal like Dante before. Now it was too late, and Demetri's pain intensified, and he wished for death. The type of death that provided a lack of existence. An eternal death. He would disappear like he never existed.

These thoughts only helped to compound Demetri's torment and if it weren't for his hatred towards Alex Dante permeating his suffering, he might ask his master for the mercy to be set free to exist no more. But he still wanted to exist. He desired that chance to encounter Alex Dante, the mortal, again. It propelled him to battle against this suffering.

Suddenly, Demetri's eyesight returned to him. It wasn't coming back immediately and fully, but rather slowly and deliberately. He was astonished to witness the return of his Viking physique as it gathered up around him. He was confused as to why this transition from spirit to physical was happening. The pain was beginning to diminish and the torment of his failure to capture Cindy Firestone and her alabaster eyes also disappeared.

His focus became more deliberate, and he was astonished to see his beloved lake and boat dock where he had so often experienced a sense of tranquility manifest itself around him. This was that mortal sanctuary that made him feel as before. When he was a revered angel of Lucifer.

This lake and dock were *his* and became the place that only a few of the demons could experience. Despite his desire for his lake, the sanctuary it offered, it had also become *his* portal back through the Abyssal and into the under realm of Hades. "Why am I here?", he wondered as his returned vision scanned the horizon?

Only a short moment ago he had been in the grips of torment. A bright light that glowed with the radiance of a thousand suns caused Demetri to cover his eyes. Fearing that Gabriel had brought him back here for more punishment came to his demon mind. The light began to diminish enough for Demetri to recognize that the keeper of this radiance was not Gabriel, but another powerful spirit, his master Lucifer. Demetri fell to his knees in reverence. He should have realized that with the absence of suffering and pain, it could only be because of his master. He did not, and could not, look upon the face of Lucifer. All he could muster was to bow his head, while crouching on the boat dock, and with a great deal of effort and a barely audible guttural voice speak his appellation, "Master".

He felt an oddly warm stroke on his golden blonde hair by two fingers that felt almost earthly and mortal. As the fingers caressed the bangs of his hair they gently moved across his forehead. With his other hand Lucifer held Demetri's chin in his palm and hoisted his head to enable their eyes to meet.

Lucifer's eyes revealed an almost gentle and forgiving look which caused Demetri to be even more confused. Lucifer was tall and thin but not devoid of an obvious muscular build. His face was handsome, like a mortal, with a smile that would draw you to him without resistance. Mortals who painted images of how Satan might appear, skin color red with horns protruding from his scalp, were gravely mistaken.

His master wore robes of silk that flowed as if a breeze were blowing them about his torso. Yet, there was no wind as the lake environment was calm and still. His master was majestic, appealing, and godly. Demetri feared to witness scorn and anger emitting from Lucifer. The fact that his master was present and showing him this kindness and compassion continued to fuel his confusion.

Satan spoke, "My dear Demetri, you and I have not communed for many earthly years."

Looking around at the boat dock, Lucifer turned his eyes away from Demetri who watched as his master's gaze careened across the landscape of the lake and surrounding banks. He had seen this look before. Lucifer's gaze was much akin to the stare of a father of one of his former conquests. This father had come to see his son's first apartment. Despite the son's pride in a place of his own, his father's look was not rewarding of the accomplishment.

Lucifer's look was just like that. The failure of that father to ever express pride towards his son, made Demetri's work all the easier in capturing that boy's soul. Demetri felt *that* pang of disappointment in the displayed look of his master. For a moment he understood how that boy felt.

"Well Demetri, far be it from me to judge why you chose this place as your sanctuary." Lucifer let go of Demetri's chin and turned his back to him as he walked along the dock towards the lake, motioning Demetri to stand and join him towards the front of the boat dock. He did as his master commanded. "I have brought you to this place and freed you from your pain and torment. You might be wondering why that is?" Lucifer spoke with an air of smugness.

Demetri most certainly was questioning *why* and more so, *why* he had been restored to his angelic prowess.

Lucifer continued, "You have been a faithful servant to me Demetri. An accomplished and persuasive angel, and unlike Gabriel's God, I do not punish my beloved servants."

Demetri struggled to recall if he had ever witnessed Gabriel's God punishing his host except when his master, Lucifer, had challenged him. He certainly was a jealous God. To now be free from the torment was enough to show Demetri why he had followed his master from his meager position as the leader of worship in his former home, to his dominion here, over earth.

"I not only show mercy for my own, but I also allow for retribution," Satan explained with an air of benevolence. "Gabriel followed you here to this, your special place, to vanquish you and reprimand you. He cast you back through the portal. That act was a violation of the sanctuary that *I* provided for you! This is not his right or does he have the authority! *IT IS MINE!*" Demetri could feel the anger and thunder in his master's voice.

With that outburst of scorn Lucifer's shoulders relaxed, and he once again turned to face Demetri with an unbecoming smile. He wished that his master would have continued their meeting without facing him. "I have resurrected you my dear Demetri. I have brought you back to harvest souls for me, and understand this one thing, Gabriel and his God shall not tamper with you, my angel, this time!"

Looking into his master's eyes, Demetri felt a surge of power he had never previously felt. It was a feeling as if

Lucifer himself had indwelled him. He understood that he had been provided a second chance by his master, his god. Lucifer held up both hands as if to command reverence from Demetri. "Now go and do not fail me in this task I have appointed for you."

He was grateful in this chance, but Demetri was also hesitant in his knowledge that it was not *only* Gabriel that he had not been able to overcome, but he had also witnessed a mortal who had shown dominion over him. Demetri mustered enough courage to ask his master about this because he honestly was not prepared to challenge or understand this earthly foe. He must learn more about this mortal, Alex Dante, and how he derived his power. He formed the words in his demon mind, and then his mouth to ask Lucifer, "Lord, you are great, and my god, but how am I to challenge the mortal, Dante if I encounter him again?"

But just as he developed the courage to speak his question it was too late, Lucifer was gone.

Chapter 2:
Encounter

HER EYES HESITANTLY SPLIT open to accept the inevitable sunlight of the morning sun. As Courtney struggled to accept the dawning of a new day, she could barely make out the image of a figure coming to sit down on the bed near her shoulder. She buried her head into the wadded-up pillow that was in the crook of her arm. "You better have brought me coffee, husband, or I want a divorce," she spoke in a muffled tone through the pillow.

Alex leaned down across her shoulder as he spoke softly into her ear, "My, oh my, how quickly love fades and your mate's true colors are exposed!" He set the cup that was nestled in his other hand, on the nightstand next to her head with just enough force as to make a thud sound that was unmistakable as being done in playful frustration. "Salted caramel creamer too. Lucky for you, I have saved this marriage and we don't have to return the blender we got as a wedding present from your aunt Marge," Alex said in a nonchalant manner.

Courtney turned her head towards her husband and smiled. Alex was infatuated by her smile. A smile that emanated from a face diverse of any makeup or assistance to enhance its beauty. He knew how lucky he was. Alex had waited for this one, his one and only, and she was certainly worth the wait. He leaned in to kiss her. The same coffee he had brought for her, that rested on the nightstand by their bed, had grown cold and untouched, long before either of them departed from their bed.

The newlyweds were just two weeks into their marriage after only a three-month engagement. They decided on Alex's quaint little Astoria home as the place where they would live. It was small, but it was all they needed right now and despite Alex becoming leery of the quality of the neighborhood, they felt it financially gave them time to eventually find a place they both could call their own.

Pastor Glen Firestone had agreed to marry them after they received a few pre-marriage counseling sessions. Alex knew it was slightly uncomfortable for Glen during these counseling sessions, knowing of Alex's extraordinary gift. Often, the counseling sessions led to Glen asking more questions about Alex's abilities, than discussing the responsibilities of a Christian husband. It had been five months since Alex's last encounter with the demon Demetri, and Glen was very inquisitive to understand just what that encounter had been like.

Describing those events and his experiences with the demon was difficult for Alex. He still struggled to understand his gift and exactly what he was meant to do with it, so he felt like he was being rude to Glen when the answers he provided to his questions were short or vague.

In the months following the events with Cindy, Alex continued to see the demon Gayland from time-to-time at the hospital. He had also seen other demons about, but they immediately received Alex's rebuke. With his reputation among the demons as being *the* mortal who defeated the powerful Demetri, they were fearful of him, and most disappeared shortly after. Even though Alex had failed to scare off Gayland, it was obvious the demon avoided him at all costs.

Courtney understood and tolerated Glen's departure from the main topic of Christian matrimony during their counseling sessions. If she was being honest, she was a bit curious about Alex's abilities to see and discuss *life* with angels and demons alike. She never pressed Alex on any spiritual encounters he might have had, unless he wanted to share them, and truth be known, Alex was as guarded in discussing these things with his beloved bride as he was with anyone.

As Alex moved from the bedroom to the bathroom to take a shower, he turned the shower faucet to the right angle to produce just the desired mix of hot and cold water. The water began its splatter upon the tile walls of the shower and as Alex prepared to enter the stall, Courtney called out from the bedroom, "What's on our agenda for today, love?"

Alex was only slightly perturbed that his bride would ask him a question as he was entering the shower because it would make an audible conversation almost impossible. He needed to answer her with a response that would hopefully elicit a careful thought and some pondering that would allow him the time to finish his shower before continuing the conversation. He thought about possibly answering with a response, "Anything you want to do Courtney!" That answer would only have solicited further shower conversation leading to frustration on Alex's part to hear Courtney. He had activities planned for their day, so he decided to just lay them out for her before sliding into his shower retreat. Alex stuck his head out from inside the bathroom and replied, "Since this is the last day of our honeymoon before we have to go back to work, I thought we could take a drive down the coast, to Seaside, do some shopping and finish off our journey with a good crab supper."

"You are such a good planner! I had the same plan, exactly. We were meant to be together," Courtney laughed. It was a beautiful day along the coast of Oregon. Not too warm, and not too cool. The couple liked to drive with the windows down so that they could take in the marine smells of the coastal shore. They held hands across the console dividing the front seats. Alex produced a subtle grin thinking to himself just how fortunate he was to have Courtney as his life partner. God had blessed him beyond measure. Since they were content not to be in heavy discussion with each other, Alex asked, "Mind if I turn on a little music?" He loved many kinds of music but had to admit he was a 70's soft rock playlist type-of-guy. The coastal highway hummed beneath them as Alex and Courtney sang the lyrics to one of their favorite songs.

"I bless the rains down in Africa. Gonna take some time to do the things we never have..."

"Best lyrics ever," Courtney said.

"Got that right," Alex agreed.

The day could not have gone better. They enjoyed each other and the town of Seaside. At the pull off from the coastal highway that overlooked the Pacific Ocean, Alex and Courtney held hands, kissed, and watched the surf slap its foam up onto the blanket of sand before it pulled back out into the ocean. The two enjoyed a typical Oregon coast seafood feast at one of their favorite restaurants on the north side of Seaside. Dungeness crab was in season and being an Oregon delicacy, they couldn't pass it up.

After finishing a long and enjoyable feast the couple was walking to their car. Alex opened her car door as she had become accustomed to from her gentleman husband. They must have come close to the restaurant's closing time because when they had arrived for dinner the parking lot had been full so they had been forced to park in the last spot on the perimeter edge. Now, most of the spots were open as the rest of the patrons had finished their dining experience and left for home. Alex walked to the front of his car after placing Courtney into the passenger side. He stopped to glance to his right at a blinking light illuminating the night sky. Next to their favorite seafood restaurant and sharing the same parking lot was a small local tavern. The sign had three neon letters that had obviously burned out and read;

OZ__Tavern

Alex could tell the sign was supposed to read Ozone Tavern, but he somehow thought it was better with the letters not lit. He proceeded walking towards his side of the car when a patron who was just arriving at the tavern brushed up against Alex's side, cutting into the path heading towards the entrance.

The figure was tall and cloaked in a dark hooded sweatshirt with the hood pulled up covering his head. Alex could not see his face as it was almost entirely masqueraded beneath the hood. Normally Alex would not have paid much attention to a casual bump of shoulders, but this encounter put Alex's senses on high alert. The figure kept walking towards the tavern without so much as an offer of apology or even to say, "excuse me". Alex stood for a long moment and stared at the back of the figure until it entered the tavern. He walked to the driver side of the car and climbed in. Putting his keys into the ignition, Alex started the car.

Courtney looked at Alex and asked, "What was that all about?"

"Not sure. Just a funny feeling. A feeling like I knew him," Alex responded.

"Did you encounter a demon?" She inquired.

"Yah," he replied so as to not provoke any more questions. On the trip back home, she noticed Alex was unusually quiet.

Chapter 3:
Back in the Game

THE TALL MYSTERIOUS FIGURE in the dark hoodie sat at the bar next to the troubled man who desperately needed another drink. Nobody noticed the hooded figure; he was invisible to the tavern patrons and staff. He studied the man very closely, watching and listening to every failure this man mumbled to himself. Demetri preferred to indwell females. He could only speculate it was because women were more complex, and provided a better challenge for him, and that was what he craved.

Males seemed to succumb so easily when taken. This made him fear he would become lazy. He would become just like Gayland. There had been very few male souls that Demetri had delivered to his master, but none that he cared to recall. Even most of the female souls he delivered were forgotten just as soon as they were released to his master. Except the woman in 1920, he thought about her often. Her spirit was raucous, just like the one he desperately wants to forget but can't. The girl with the alabaster eyes.

He was nervous and hesitant even though this loser was obviously easy pickings. Demetri needed a quick triumph. He needed to get back his confidence. He had finally been challenged by a host and, with the aid of

Gabriel and a mortal, he had lost that challenge. His *only* loss. If it weren't for the mercy of his master he wouldn't even be sitting here, resurrected, and ready to possess again.

As Demetri entered the mind and body of Luke Berringer, he felt invigorated. He felt and filled Luke through and through. This was nothing like his experience with Cindy. He knew now that he *never* really had her, not fully. What was missing with the indwelling of Cindy was all here with Luke. He felt Luke's hand across his face. He felt him rub his greasy hair from front to back and place his ball cap on his head. Perhaps he would lead Luke to his beloved lake and boat dock and have his drunken body fall from the dock so Demetri might feel the water engulf him as Luke drowned. Nobody would miss this soul! Demetri could end this one quickly, and while doing so, he might get to enjoy the cold and wetness of the lake water as *this* soul expired.

He understood now that he was just a little jealous of mortals. He smirked over this thought. How could a mighty angel with the full authority of Lucifer, the living deity of all mortals, be jealous?

Luke realized his night of drinking at the Ozone Tavern was over. The bartender gave him an emphatic *"NO"* when he plead for just one more. Despite his difficulty in getting off his barstool and stumbling towards the exit he knew he wasn't done drinking for the night. He still felt the pain of his failures and suddenly, despite the amount he had already drank, those failures seemed to haunt him now more than when the evening started. He needed the whiskey as long as he could still feel the pain of how his wife, Stephanie, who had lost all faith in him as a husband, a husband who could not provide for her and their unborn child, had left him. At least until the pain was gone.

He had lost his business as one of the best salmon fishing sport guides on the coast of Oregon because he couldn't quit drinking with his buddies. She hated him, and it was her fault he drank. She expected too much from him. Demetri rejoiced at this rage and anger dwelling inside his new host.

"Luke, you and I are going to find that bottle. You are not done drinking tonight, son," Demetri reassured his new subject like a parent who had promised a puppy to a child!

Stumbling to the Silverado truck that his father had let him use until he got back on his feet, Luke fumbled in his drunken state for the keys. After several clumsy attempts he was able to start the truck. Backing the truck in a jerky fashion and almost hitting a concrete parking block, he was able to put the truck in drive and pull out onto the deserted roadway.

After driving a short distance Luke became a bit panicked as he became coherent enough to realize it was too late for any liquor stores to be open. Demetri injected a demented thought into Luke's head, "If the liquor store ain't open, well then, I'll just make it open!"

Chapter 4:
Purpose

HE TOSSED AND TURNED FOR SEVERAL HOURS before finally succumbing to the realization that sleep was not going to come easy tonight. Alex considered his restlessness could be because he just wasn't ready to go back to work. His wedding and honeymoon had been the best time of his life.

Slowly getting out of bed, Alex pulled on his robe and tied it around his waist. He carefully made his way out of the bedroom and closed the door behind him as to not wake up Courtney. He tip-toed to the kitchen, opened the refrigerator and found a cold bottle of water in the door. Sitting at their small kitchen table, Alex screwed the cap off the bottle, and took a small sip.

His mind was racing with the thoughts of seeing his patients in the morning and he couldn't help but feel anticipation about having some time to visit with Cindy. Through all that had happened between them and their battle with Demetri, they certainly had formed a bond with each other, much like a brother and sister.

Alex was eager to discuss with Cindy that very experience. He was slightly worried he might upset Cindy and provoke a relapse in her recovery, but he laughed to himself about this thought. Since her triumph over

Demetri, she had shown everyone, including her doctors, that her delusions were under control. The doctor's prided themselves on their therapies of giving her coping skills and took most of the credit for her recovery, but Alex knew *how* and *why* she was showing so much improvement. Cindy had been moved to a less restrictive ward at the hospital, so Alex was no longer responsible for her care. He still escorted her on walks whenever his schedule allowed, and he cherished those moments because she was instrumental in Alex's attempt to try and understand his connection to another dimension. A dimension filled with fallen angels.

When Alex and Courtney were married, Cindy was able to attend their wedding with special court permission. It required a GPS ankle bracelet and an escort, that often was the same person responsible for filling in for Alex when he was absent for those visits with Cindy. This surrogate escort was none other than the youth pastor at Seaside Community Church, Tyler McIntyre.

Tyler was 6" 2" tall with a muscular build which he had developed playing linebacker for Trinity College. He had graduated with a Bachelor's Degree in Pastoral Studies. With an obvious receding hair line for such a young man of 29 years, Tyler had opted to abandon all hair. With his build. he carried the baldness just fine.

Tyler had become a frequent flyer at the hospital, and it was obvious to Alex, that he and Cindy were infatuated with each other. He was happy for both and could easily understand why Tyler had become smitten with her. She had put on weight in all the right places, eclipsing the emaciation that had manifested from the wear of the drugs. Despite the scars that would forever be part of her legacy, her beauty shined through and helped to hide their presence. Cindy had confided during one of her visits with Alex that the physical scars of her prior life didn't bother her. When people commented about them, she was happy to tell them about her salvation, albeit sans of discussing her bout with a demon impersonating as her dead ex-boyfriend. Still, with all the thoughts that returning to work conjured within Alex, he sensed that was not the reason he was feeling the apprehension and anxiety here in the wee hours of the morning.

He wanted to go to bed and sleep, knowing the rigors of returning to work tomorrow would require him to be at the top of his game. Alex began to rub his eyes vigorously, as if that would somehow ease his tension and provide some comfort to allow peace and slumber. Once refocused on the kitchen surrounding him, his heart skipped a beat causing him to topple the water bottle in front of him. Sitting across from Alex, sporting a casual posture with his hands resting on his lap and one leg crossed over the other, was his old friend and accomplice, George Bingham.

Alex picked up the water bottle, which fortunately had the cap screwed on tight enough as to not have spilled the contents, and spoke in an exasperated manner, "Holy Cow George, you Angels sure have a knack of showing up when you're least expected!"

"Sorry for my sudden appearance and startling you my dear friend. I understand this is an odd hour for you, but it is a needed visit from me."

As he began to reclaim his composure, Alex's face produced a broad smile. "I've missed you and I have so many questions," Alex said in an impatient and excited manner. "First, I know you look like my friend George, but what, or should I say *who*, shall I call you? I mean no disrespect to you, as I know you are the Archangel Gabriel, but somehow, I feel I should pay proper reverence to you."

George laughed at Alex's question. "Oh, I could appear before you as I truly am, but as you know, I am a spiritual creation. I am not of flesh and blood. Appearing before you in this manner, as this being, is more comfortable for *you*. And aside from bringing you comfort in seeing me like this, I have become rather fond of this mortal image," George chuckled as he perused his appearance. "And that is why I am here Alex, my friend, to bring you comfort from our Father. He brings you the peace of knowledge for the purpose you will serve.

Alex, despite having the privilege of sitting across the table from the Archangel Gabriel who had manifested himself as a short, slightly obese, older man who had all the answers and wisdom of the ages, he felt compelled to bow his head and pray and offer praise to the God of the Universe. It was then that all connection with his earthly domain ceased, and the Lord spoke directly to Alex with no interruption surrounding them.

Chapter 5:
Acts

STANDING IN FRONT OF ONE of the darkened windows of Seaside's largest liquor store, Luke stared at the flashing red neon sign that read, "CLOSED". Despite his current state of inebriation, Luke's focus was guided by Demetri to a flower planter that was between the parking lot and liquor store, and he was able to steady himself enough to pick up a large rock from the planter.

Stumbling forward, Luke could make out the objects of his desire just on the other side of one window. It was definitely a display stand full of various brands of whisky. He couldn't make out what brands they were, but Luke wasn't concerned about that. At this point he wasn't about to be picky. All that stood between him, and the whiskey bottles, were a rock and a window.

Licking his lips, he took one last glance behind him to confirm his truck was running and the door to the driver's side was wide open, understanding that a quick getaway would be required. Luke focused on the rock in his right hand, made a wind up like a major league pitcher and with as much strength as he had, threw the rock at the large window. It shattered into a thousand pieces just as he had planned. Luke moved carefully forward with as much care as a drunken man could, trying to miss any of the larger jagged pieces of broken glass. Reaching in, he grabbed the two bottles of whiskey that were closest to him and in a zig-zag motion stumbled back to his truck.

Tossing the bottles into the cab on the front seat, he shut the door, threw the transmission into drive and with tires screeching Luke drove out of the liquor store parking lot, over an elevated curb, and out onto Main Street.

Demetri could not recall being this invigorated. He had underestimated this human and just how sinisterly he could be manipulated. With whiskey now sitting on the truck seat beside him, Luke slowed his speed as he wound his truck down a poorly lit residential street looking for a place to park, turn off his engine, and drink his pain into oblivion.

Off in the distance Luke could hear the sounds of sirens. Screaming, wailing sirens. Up the street was a dimly lit property with large elms that hung their branches well out and over the street. This looked like the perfect secluded spot. It was as if his truck belonged here. The single wide trailer perched on the property was dark and void of any activity.

Luke managed to pull the truck over, shift it into park and turn off the engine. He waited a few minutes just to make sure he hadn't stirred any of the residents on this street. When he was confident that he was undetected, he pulled one of the bottles towards him and removed the cap that guarded the golden-brown distilled liquid he needed. The last thing that Luke thought he would recall before he passed out was his wife's face. It was a distorted face of one who had been crying. He felt no ease of pain. The content of the bottle brought him no solace. His wife's cries haunted him as he passed out.

Demetri took no delight from her cries either. In fact, he felt tinges of torment that he shouldn't have felt at all. He was perplexed by this. The torment he felt was the same as he had experienced prior to his master removing it from him. The twinge of pain was temporary, gone as quickly as it came. Although Luke had not gained any element of consciousness, Demetri caught a glimpse of a figure outside of the truck window. He struggled to sense who it might be that had discovered his host and was looking directly at him. *"Who are you,"* Demetri quizzically thought?

The figure turned from the truck window and began to slowly move away. As it did, Demetri acknowledged that it was a very young boy. Not yet a toddler and somehow devoid of any form, but a young boy, nonetheless. A second figure was lurking behind the boy. Demetri hadn't noticed the second figure until they turned to move away. The second figure was holding the boy. In fact, the boy was being carried as a father would his young child. Upon noticing this second figure the pain in Demetri's eyes intensified. He felt powerless. This was like nothing he had ever felt before in his moments of torment. But then he remembered, it was precisely the same pain he had felt when he lost Cindy.

Chapter 6:
Communion

GABRIEL, WHO HAD TAKEN THE IMAGE OF GEORGE, watched patiently as Alex lifted his head from his communion with God. "It's a magnificent gift, isn't it?" Gabriel questioned Alex.

Alex was unable to answer. His mind and thoughts were racing. He sat and stared at Gabriel until he collected a sense of the reality around him. Once his mind had returned mentally to his meager Astoria kitchen, a smile as wide as the Grand Canyon appeared on his face along with a feeling of euphoria. Finally composed enough to speak, Alex answered, "I am so humbled before him. I am so blessed to believe and worship him. This…this ability along with the knowledge he has provided me, has made me so…so."

"Humble," Gabriel laughed.

"Yes, humble," Alex smiled and chuckled as he replied.

"Our Lord has explained to you the work you have been called to do," Gabriel responded with all knowledge and affirmation.

Alex felt a peace deep inside him that only the comfort of The Lord could have provided. He knew that in time, he could share with Courtney the journey he went on tonight. His sojourn to find answers, and with those answers, an understanding of how he fit into all of this. He now understood the figure that he literally ran into last night. That accidental bump in the restaurant parking lot, was none other than the demon Demetri. Now Alex knew the part that Demetri would play in his future, and the revelation of why this evil demon was allowed to return to *this* earth.

Demetri had no clue how a mortal man like Dante, a man that was flawed in so many ways, was anointed to battle his demon kind, and why this common mortal could not lose. Being a spawn of Hell, he certainly didn't comprehend that Alex was wearing the full armor of God, and part of that armor, was a host of Angels.

George looked Alex squarely in the eyes and leaned across the table to whisper in his ear, "I know now you will sleep Alex. As you must. You have much to do and yet, even though I leave you for now, I will not leave here before I get a cup of your coffee!"

Alex laughed as George's infamous, stained cup materialized out of nowhere. He stood, grasped the coffee pot, and walked to the sink to fill it with water.

Chapter 7:
Mt. Sinai

SHE STUDIED ALEX'S FACE AS HE DROVE. His look was different than she had ever seen before. She tried to stare at him without raising his suspicion, but it was too obvious. Alex knew exactly what she was doing.

"What...why are you looking at me like that?" Alex questioned.

Courtney turned her gaze from him, but she knew she had been caught. She felt obliged to answer even though she found it difficult to put into words. "Do you recall that sermon by Pastor Glen when he preached about Moses when he received the Ten Commandments?" was the only thing she could reference to explain her stare.

"Sure, of course I remember," Alex responded with the curiosity of a cat.

"Well, when Moses came off Mount Sinai and his wife, Zipporah, saw him for the first time after he heard God's voice, that's how you look now. Just like Moses!"

"I guess my face can't hide what has happened to me. Just like with Zipporah, you have sensed that a miracle has occurred," Alex responded in marvel of the intuition of his wife. Pulling the car over to the side of the road, he put the car in park and shifted his body to face her directly. Alex

25

had a very serious demeanor as he spoke to Courtney. "I have many things to reveal to you, honey. So many things that are miraculous. I don't mean to be so mysterious with you but my story of what happened to me last night deserves more time than we have this morning. I promise once we get home tonight, I will share every fantastic detail with you."

"Promise?" Courtney asked seeking a commitment.

"Promise!" Alex answered in reaffirmation.

Alex shifted the car back into drive and they continued their journey to the hospital. Getting out of the car, he continued his practice of opening Courtney's door. He grabbed her and brought her close. They kissed and grabbed their belongings for the workday. As they entered the security port at the hospital Alex secretly wished it would be George sitting there, smiling, and telling him their coffee break would be much needed today. He was a bit disappointed that it wasn't George.

Courtney and Alex passed through the portal and separated at the junction as Alex headed towards Ward Fifteen. As they split, Courtney called out to him with a question, "I'm not going to lose you to the Hebrews, am I?"

"Not a chance Zipporah, not a chance," Alex answered sarcastically as he headed down the hallway not looking back at her. He stowed his lunch and thermos is his locker and took a quick trip down memory lane. His memories took him to his previous encounter with Gayland in this room, and how that encounter was just the beginning of his journey with the spirit world. Alex composed himself and walked out of the breakroom to relieve his co-worker, Alan.

After receiving the pass-along news from Alan, information which was usually not earth shattering, Alex bid goodbye to his Ward Fifteen cohort. As Alan headed out of the ward he said, "Hey, I forgot to tell you congratulations."

"I appreciate that buddy," Alex replied.

"By the way, I think your wife is *hot*," Alan laughed.

Alex smiled and waved him out of the ward. He had never thought Alan was particularly bright but, based on his comment, he was beginning to reconsider. Steven Sinclair was sitting up in his bed when Alex brought him some new toiletries for his bathroom. Upon seeing Alex, Mr. Sinclair got a stern look on his face and began to shake his index finger at him. "Know this young man, I shall never let you have extended time off again. The valet you retained to assist me was incapable of addressing my most subtle needs!"

Alex bowed to Mr. Sinclair and replied, "I'm sorry sir. I realize what an inconvenience my absence must have been for you. Fortunately, I shall only take a bride once in my life, so it shan't be repeated."

"Oh, yes, your imprisonment," Steven croaked! Mr. Sinclair continued their conversation stating that he would be meeting with the Queen this morning as it had been long overdue due to Alex's absence. "I simply could not meet with her majesty without my valet here to assist me!"

"Very good sir. I'm glad to be back in your service," Alex nodded as he spoke.

"Oh, and word is Mr. Churchill might be attending this morning also," Sinclair responded.

Alex couldn't help but love this old man. Despite being scolded by an English nobleman who had never set foot in England, he cherished their relationship. He thought it was much more entertaining to be scolded by Steven Sinclair than having to deal with the demon world! That thought was quickly strengthened as Alex moved to the rooms that housed criminal patients. Alex stepped into the room that at one time contained his friend Cindy Firestone, and the infamous Demetri.

Looking around, Alex found his mind wandering to the events that led to his helping to save Cindy's earthly life and eternal soul. Now with all that had occurred since, hearing God's voice and beginning to understand what God has planned for him, he couldn't help but recall his moments with Demetri.

He understood he would encounter Demetri again. Next time it would be different. Still, as with many things, you must crawl before you can walk. He turned from the room and decided he had spent enough time reminiscing and envisioning the future.

Spending the rest of his shift attending to his patients and reacquainting himself with their nuances, he looked up at the clock and rejoiced to know his relief would soon be there. Alex heard the electronic mechanism at the door deactivate, allowing Alan to enter Ward Fifteen and shortly thereafter he was standing next to Alex, ready to receive his shift ending pass- on. Gathering his belongings, Alex made his way towards the pneumatic door that allowed exit from the ward. He scanned his access card, opening the door and allowing him to escape to a quieter place. As Alex walked through the door he called out to Alan, "See you in the morning. I'm going home to be with my *hot* wife!"

Both men laughed.

Chapter 8:
Reveal

ON THE DRIVE HOME Alex could tell that Courtney was eager for him to reveal those circumstances that were responsible for having led him away from his usual casual manner to this current state of seriousness. He didn't want to torture her by having to wait after dinner was prepared, the meal eaten and the dishes washed, before they could relax with each other, so he offered to stop at one of their favorite local pizza places and pick up dinner.

Courtney was anxious to discuss the events that visibly showed on her husband, but she was equally tired after working her first day after coming back from the most amazing event thus far in her lifetime, the marriage to her soulmate. She readily agreed to the pizza idea. After reaching home, Courtney kicked off her shoes and made a beeline for the sofa where she flew to drown her body in the depths of the cushions and pillows. "Hey, my love, can you grab me a soda and a slice of pizza? I'm much too exhausted to move from this couch," Courtney sheepishly implored.

Alex responded, "I guess I had better serve you. All the guys at work think you're hot and I don't want to jeopardize my position here."

As they both laughed over Alex's response, he served up a slice of pizza for each of them, placed them on paper plates and grabbed a couple of cold sodas from the refrigerator. Alex handed her a plate and he sat down beside her and took a bite of his pizza knowing that very soon their conversation would turn serious.

Courtney began to speak first with a mouthful of pizza, "So, tell me, who are all these men at work that think I'm hot?" She had a way of relieving the tension between them. The humor soothed Alex and let him collect his thoughts in preparation to tell his bride of his miraculous experience. He would not make her wait any longer and began his story of how he had been unable to sleep and went to the kitchen where he encountered George. Her mouth dropped and she was flabbergasted and amused as he told his story about a magnificent Angel like Gabriel, who preferred to manifest himself to Alex as frumpy old George.

As Alex spoke, Courtney became entranced like an unsuspecting patron at a local carnival getting drawn in by a mystic. She followed each expression on his face. This was uncharted territory for their relationship. He continued to explain that he was unable to stay focused on his conversation with George and fell into what he believed was a trance. "That's when it happened," he said.

"What happened?" Courtney eagerly inquired.

"I heard God's voice."

He went on to explain that it was not like a man's voice. It wasn't English either, but he understood every word. God told him that he has been anointed to be the witness *for* those spiritual forces that come from the Abyssal, the portal from hell. "To be," he searched for the right word, "the *keeper* between what God created and the realm from which they come. Satan himself will know of *me* because I will have authority over his legion of demons. I will bear witness to those demons that it is the God of Heaven that allows them to tempt mortals because of free will, and soon all will come to declare that very truth, themselves. God declared to me that I must wear his full armor when Satan comes for me, because he will come *at* me!

At this point he became very thoughtful and sullen in his next statement and spoke very carefully. "I am, and will be, as we near the end of the age of man, the keeper of the very pathway that Satan and his legions will be cast down."

Courtney looked into Alex's eyes. Despite being afraid of what her husband had just shared with her, she saw a look of encouragement and reverence. She spoke calmly, "Then you are like Moses. You have a job to do for our Lord. You will be the voice to deliver God's message." Courtney knew he was not chosen to lead men as a prophet, he would have authority over fallen angels in their final defeat. He would be God's witness for the demons.

She curled up within the comfort of her husband's embrace. All of this was beyond her comprehension, but she knew she had a part to play in this spiritual battle. That age-old battle of good versus evil, was upon them. Courtney hugged him tight and right there on the couch, they both fell asleep.

As she slept, Courtney dreamed. She is visited by a beautiful young woman. She is impressed by the woman's natural beauty but understands she isn't a modern woman. Her hair is brunette, but it is difficult to tell how long because she wears it up and pinned behind her. Her dress is dark and full length and trimmed tightly to her petite waistline, which is most likely aided by a corset. Still, Courtney can tell her figure is ample and feminine. Her eyes are deep blue, and her facial features are very similar to someone Courtney has seen before, but she can't recall whom it might be.

The woman curtsies before Courtney, which is a foreign greeting in today's age, and introduces herself, "My name is Annabel, Annabel Perkins. I have come to visit you so that you may know who and what I am. I was born in Portland, Oregon in the year 1900. I died in 1920 by my own hand."

Courtney noticed what appeared to be scars on the woman's wrists.

"I was a woman of the night. That was my profession. My story is one of despair as I had no worth on earth. I laid with any man or woman that would pay me to do so. My mother died when I was young girl, and I never knew my father. From a very young age, my body was my tender."

Courtney was saddened by the tale that this woman told and questioned why she haunted her? Even though her profession should have dealt a blow to her appearance, Courtney reveled in Annabel's beauty. Annabel continued her story, "I sought love. Not physical love, but somebody who would see my worth. Someone who could value my soul. It was not a human that brought *that* love to me. It was something else!"

Courtney asked, "What was it?"

Tears welled up in Annabel's eyes, "It possessed me top to bottom. It filled my body and my mind with promises that we would be together for eternity. If I ended my earthly life!" Annabel pointed to a bathtub that had just appeared behind her in Courtney's dream. "I climbed into that tub and used a straight razor to cut deep into each of my wrists. I laid there with my eyes closed and waited for peace, and love, to engulf me as my blood spilled from me. It was then that I heard a voice that startled me. I opened my eyes and standing before me gazing at my nakedness without the lust that I usually witnessed in my life, was a tall, beautiful creature of massive build. He cried out that he could not stay with me. His master would soon collect me. This figure then lowered himself to his knees and tried to reach out to me. He extended his hand and then retracted it, as if he was in pain."

Annabel bowed her head so Courtney could not see her eyes. "He then spoke to me, I am Demetri, an angel of Lucifer and I cannot love a mortal. I cannot stay with you or be with you. It is not allowed for my kind, and now I must leave. With that declaration, he was gone, and I had been deceived," Annabel spoke now lifting her head so Courtney could see her ghostly eyes.

She explained that at that moment she knew she would die and never know true love. His *was* love she had felt. It was not the type she craved, love that needed her, not for pleasure, but to be with her and dwell within her. But Demetri had lied to her. *His* love had been a false excursion.

Then a light appeared before her, and Annabel thought for a moment that it might be Demetri, that he had returned to perpetuate more of his demon lies upon her. She wouldn't put it beyond his cruelty to do so. Then this light which was devoid of form, spoke to her and she felt a love and peace that Demetri had never provided for her. At first Annabel was skeptical. She trusted nobody, but this light reached out to her and touched her in a way she knew was different. Annabel knew for the first time that she had received the truth.

"The light was God?" Courtney asked.

"Yes, the light was Jesus. The lies and deception Demetri offered, were fulfilled and made true by my Lord, I died on earth that day in that bathtub, but my spirit lives because at the brink of my earthly death, my eternal soul was redeemed. I come to you tonight, in *your* dream, so you may know me. I offer myself in the service of the keeper, your husband, Alex. He shall battle Lucifer, soon."

Courtney gasped!

"Our Lord has brought me to you so you will know that myself and the Angels, are his servants. We will protect and encourage him. "Also know this, Demetri will be used by Satan to try and lure Alex to him. This will be folly. When the time comes, I will be there to assist your husband in his confrontation with Lucifer himself. I will be quite handy at that moment."

With that comment, Annabel left Courtney's dream and she woke up to find she was still in the embrace of her husband's arms. Before she fell back asleep, she thought about Annabel. It occurred to her then, why Annabel had seemed so familiar. The resemblance was striking. Annabel looked very much like Cindy Firestone. As she dozed off, she whispered to her husband, "*WE* battle not flesh and blood."

Courtney had no more dreams that night and slept in the protection of her husband's arms and those of the Angels and saints.

Chapter 9:
Sunlight

THE LIGHT OF DAY WAS PAINFUL, and Luke squinted while trying to gain focus on the world before him. The pain in his head didn't help him, in any way, to greet the day. He'd had hangovers before but this one was horrible. Luke felt like he was going to vomit and reached out, pulled the driver's side door handle and quickly exited the truck.

Stumbling around he looked quickly for a bush or tree to hide behind to release the contents of his stomach. Finding a short cinder block wall Luke fell to his knees and puked. He spat and wiped the remnants from his mouth as best he could. Luke wanted to feel well enough to crawl back and get behind the wheel of the truck, start the engine, put it into gear and drive home to ask Stephanie for forgiveness. His wish was shattered when a voice boomed out from behind him commanding, "**Get on the ground. Get on the ground, now!**"

Demetri couldn't believe Luke would let himself get caught in this position. Perhaps he had over-estimated that this subject would let this happen. He must be losing his touch in picking souls and perhaps he did not deserve this second chance. He had been clumsy and would face sure banishment to the under-realm and experience an eternity of torture. Perhaps he deserved it. The scene of the small child and the figure that carried him away from the truck window just a few hours ago, shook Demetri to his core. Still, he was out of excuses to justify this predicament and he had to think fast.

The police officers each grabbed Luke under one of his arms and hoisted his handcuffed body off the ground to carry him to the waiting patrol car. They set Luke in the back of the patrol car, and he could see the wetness of his own vomit on his plaid shirt. He questioned for a short moment if that was indeed what he was seeing and began to weep. Rock bottom had come to Seaside, Oregon, and Luke was living there.

The patrol car left the scene with Luke and Demetri heading towards the Seaside Oregon Detention Facility. Demetri thought to himself, "This isn't the plan. It just won't do."

Luke was called out of his holding cell in the Booking Unit and was escorted to the general population area of the jail. He still didn't feel well but at least his need to throw-up was gone. Later that morning, Luke, in an orange jumpsuit, stood before a court judge on a television monitor. He was advised that he was being charged with one count of robbery, criminal trespass, and DUI. His impromptu public defender recommended that Luke plead not guilty to hopefully solicit a good plea bargain from the District Attorney. The plea was entered, and Luke's bond was set at $35,000 total for all three charges. Upon hearing the bond amount, Luke knew he would be in jail for a very long time.

Demetri fretted, "This is getting way too complicated, He was supposed to just quickly drink himself to death, be passed to my master, and I get some time at my lake, in peace, to remember my Annabel."

1920

This mortal was different. He wished he had not indwelled this woman. In what was his job, his mission, to deliver these down-trodden souls for *his* eternal service, she had flipped everything and possessed him. Demetri gazed at her nakedness as she reclined in the tub that held her spilled blood. Since he had no mortal desires, he had no lust. He watched her as the mortal weights of this earthly realm began to be lifted from her.

These months that he had been within her had shown him a different side of mortality. Annabel had wanted to feel as though she had "worth" to someone. The sexual encounters she experienced apparently provided none of the desired worth she sought. It made Demetri glad that, as angels, they did not have to deal with such pettiness as physical love. She had shown him that mortals and angels, like himself, needed to be needed!

Her sullen eyes opened just enough to look upon his physical manifestation. That look was one that would never escape him. It shattered him to his core. He saw into her soul, and it exposed that he had betrayed her. She knew it and he knew it. He had done his job well turning her mortal desires for redemption into the tool he would use to deliver her soul.

Being his master's chief demon had its rewards. *His* lake and dock. The tranquility and peace he had once felt as an angel of the host could only be remotely felt at *his* lake. Still, he would give it all up to remain with her. "Why?" he thought. Demetri felt fear at this moment. The fear he felt was something foreign to him. Jealousy.

Present Day

Demetri had grown tired of suicide as the means to deliver his product. It made him feel lazy! With Luke in jail, it would have to be the same old thing. He would have to push Luke's mind towards ending his life. Demetri wished he had the authority to just kill Luke himself, but he had always been commanded that he must be patient, and someday that wish would be granted and provided to him, by his master.

He wondered what it would be like to destroy a mortal. Be the powerful angel that he knew he was. Patience must be practiced, and Demetri knew he had rules and must abide by them.

Luke sat in his cell alone. His knees were tucked up to his chest as he interlaced his fingers around his legs to keep them in place. His head was slouched down, and his thoughts would not, and could not, let him rest. Over the intercom of his cell a voice from the guard tower rang out. "Berringer, you have a visit!"

Luke unraveled his body, placed his feet into his jail slippers and slid off the bunk. The guard opened his cell door so he could exit towards the visiting corridor. As Luke walked towards the visit area, he imagined it would be his father on the other side of the glass holding the phone receiver. He was prepared to face the noise from his father saying how disappointed he was and how his trust had been defiled. He knew his father couldn't fail to remind him how much it cost to get *his* truck out of impound.

The guard electronically popped the door open so Luke could sit down and conduct his twenty-minute visit. Sitting on the other side of the shatterproof glass was his wife, Stephanie. Luke didn't expect to see her sitting there. He sat down and settled himself in the plastic chair facing her. His hand trembled as he brought the receiver to his ear. He had never been so embarrassed and couldn't lift his eyes to meet hers. He really didn't know what to say and fumbled to find any words. "Hey Steph, I didn't expect to see you," Luke said in a tongue-tied fashion.

"Didn't the guards tell you that I scheduled a visit for today?" Stephanie inquired.

"They probably did but my mind wanders in here," Luke replied.

He let his shoulder hold the receiver to his ear as he used one hand to brush his unkempt hair away from his face. Luke was embarrassed to talk to his wife, and she could sense that in his body language.

"Look at me Luke!" Stephanie implored him as a parent would scold a disobedient child. "I know you don't want to see me, but we need to talk."

Lifting his eyes to meet hers he expected to see nothing but disappointment and scorn in her eyes. He had done so much to earn that type of look from her, and he could never recover any dignity while why he was in this place. "I don't like it in here. I wish I could come home," Luke implored.

"I know that is what you want, but maybe this is the best place for you right now. Maybe you can find the help to get your head on straight."

Luke knew deep down that this place was the worst opportunity he had to feel better. It seemed the voices in his head kept telling him what a loser he was, and they were getting worse in here. Hoping to try and move the conversation away from his inadequateness as a husband, Luke stood up off his plastic chair and leaned forward to try and glance down at his wife's body through the glass barrier. "How is the pregnancy going? Stand up so I can see your belly. Shouldn't you be starting to show by now?"

It didn't take a rocket scientist to understand that he had just turned the conversation down a wrong path. Tears erupted from Stephanie's eyes and her sobs shook her shoulders. Luke knew instantly what she was going to reveal. 'There is no more baby, Luke." Stephanie looked up at Luke with her eyes swollen and red.

"Wha...what happened?" Luke asked.

Still sobbing, Stephanie angrily blurted out at her husband, "What do you think happened? My husband goes on a drunken bender, I have no idea where he is, he could be dead, I don't know! The doctor said it's almost impossible to know why somebody miscarries, but he was sure my stress level didn't help!"

Luke had no response for her. Deep inside his mind, the loss of his child was being played for all it was worth, by Demetri. "Do they know if the baby was a girl or a boy?" Luke reluctantly asked, knowing it would come across as insensitive.

"It was a boy," she answered.

"A boy," Demetri thought as he pondered those words in his demon brain several times. Demetri couldn't help but think back to the young child's face he saw staring at Luke through the truck window. That face was male. A boy child. He was perplexed, trying to understand that if that was the passing soul of this man's child, looking at the man who killed him, his own father, then who was the spirit that carried him?

"Your visit time is up Ms. Berringer," a voice echoed through the intercom. Stephanie arose to leave the visiting booth.

"Will you come to see me again?" Luke asked hopefully.

"I'm not sure," Stephanie answered in a way that clearly revealed the conflict in her mind and soul. Then, she walked out the door.

For the first time in a long time Luke thought about a plan. A plan to join his son and torture his family no more. Demetri was astonished by this thought because it was not placed there by him. He had grown tired of using suicide to complete his assignments but, he had to admit, this one could go there completely on its own.

Chapter 10:
The Way and the Means

HOW TO DO IT IS THE DILEMMA that confronted Luke. Opportunities and the means to end one's life were difficult to accomplish in jail. Getting enough drugs to do the deed was almost impossible, and to get any drugs at all would require money, which was something he had none of.

He looked around for a way to hang himself, but that idea also seemed out of reach.

"Ask the inmates in your pod if they have any ideas on how to kill yourself," Demetri implanted in Luke's mind.

Glancing around, Luke was not inspired by the quality of inmates that shared his same dayroom hours in this jail unit. Most of them were in custody for minor charges and awaiting court, so seeking suicide advice from these goons was probably not a solution. Luke chuckled to himself about the irony of someone that is in jail seeking knowledge about how to commit a criminal act but there wasn't a worthy criminal to be found. Feeling depressed, Luke retreated to the bunk in his cell. The pneumatic door closed behind him, and he fell asleep.

Demetri was getting tired and weary of this subject and wished for a speedy end so he could move on. Luke had become boring to him. He felt he was as much in jail as his host. This feeling was unlike *his* female hosts, Annabel, and Cindy, who constantly challenged him in every way. Even the powerful Demetri was perplexed on how this soul could be delivered. Then, the answer walked through the cell door.

Luke rolled over onto his side when he heard the door open. A tall, scrawny man with several tattoos and looking a bit disheveled entered the cell carrying his blankets and sheets. The man placed his bedding onto the bunk opposite of Luke and began to make up his bed. "Hey," the man greeted Luke with a casual greeting of two strangers.

Luke responded with a tentative "hey" back to the fellow. Not knowing how to play the game when new inmates were brought into the jail, Luke sat up and offered his new cellmate a friendlier hello. He extended his hand towards the man and said, "I'm Luke, Luke Berringer."

The newest member of the cell block extended his fist in a friendly bumping manner and replied, "Mike, my name is Mike."

Over the next three hours the two cell mates said very little to each other. Luke thought this man seemed very hard and conditioned to a life behind bars. He decided that it wasn't such a bad thing that this guy wasn't very friendly or talkative because Luke didn't feel overly eager to develop a lifelong friendship in this joint.

The evening meal was served which was never tantalizing to the pallet. Meals were generally consumed by inmates in their cells. Mike aggressively consumed his food. Luke assumed he must not have eaten recently and was extremely hungry. He kept a subtle watch on Mike and found it a little humorous to watch Mike practically lick his tray like a dog seeking every morsel. Feeling sorry for the starvation his roommate seemed to be experiencing, Luke, having lost his appetite, asked Mike if he would like to have the rest of the beans and cornbread off his tray.

"Sure, hand it on over. Waste not, want not," Mike eagerly extended his hands to accept the gift. From that point forward Mike became Luke's best friend in the jail. He shared with Luke that he was in jail until his case was settled and dropped. He explained that he was here from the Department of Corrections where he was doing seven to ten years for burglary. He had an unresolved assault charge in this County, but most likely the District Attorney would drop the charge or reduce it to a lesser charge or hopefully time served.

"What is prison like?" Luke inquired of Mike.

"Shoot brother, you never been to prison?"

Luke answered, "No, in fact, this is my first time in jail."

Mike laughed at Luke's response and queried. "Whad ya do to have the pleasure this time? Beat your old lady or something?"

Despite the fact he didn't appreciate Mike's question and how it was asked, Luke decided to take the low road. He figured it was much more tolerable with Mike being this way than saying nothing.

"I robbed a liquor store," Luke answered.

Mike let out a cackle so loud that they probably heard him in the next county. He stood up and started patting Luke on the back. "Heck boy, I've robbed at least a dozen liquor stores in my day. You ain't gonna do no hard time for that. How much money you get, twenty bucks or so?"

Luke rubbed the top of his head and offered in almost embarrassed manner, "Just two bottles of rot gut."

Mike must have laughed for a good half an hour before finally settling down so Luke could continue their conversation. "When I asked what prison is like...I was curious...you ever see anybody kill themselves in there?" Luke pressed.

"Good boy," Demetri's interest perked up at the question.

A quiet seriousness fell over cellmate Mike's face after hearing the question. "Sure, I've seen dude's end it. Why you wanna know that?"

Turning his head away from Mike, Luke began to nonchalantly flip the pages of a book he had selected from the unit's book cart. "Just curious Mike. I've just heard that guys that are going to prison, having to do hard time…well some, you know, can't do the time."

Mike shrugged off that there might have been ulterior motives to Luke's question and began to boast of his suicide knowledge in both prison and jail environments. After listening to the plethora of options available, Luke determined that of all the options, using his bed sheet, tearing it to form strips to fashion a rope would be the best suggestion. With this type of rope, he could wait until he was alone, tie it around an upper bunk that was unoccupied, and let gravity do the job.

"Yes, yes I like that idea," Demetri affirmed in Luke's mind. It was like his plan for Cindy. In a way, he wished for this same plan to be successful this time to validate him.

Later that evening Luke began to work on his handmade rope using strips of his bed sheet. He knew the damage to his sheet would eventually be discovered by the guards, but his hope was that it would be too late, and he would be with his son.

"Yes, you will be at peace and together with your son," Demetri drummed into his mind.

Luke was enjoying the peace and quiet since Mike had left the cell to go to the recreation yard. He was glad to have the experience and knowledge of incarceration that Mike brought to the table, but right now, he would rather be alone. Worried that a guard might investigate the cell and discover his project, Luke was careful to keep his rope hidden as much as possible. One of the guards came on the intercom that fed into Luke's cell and spoke, making him jump. "Hey Berringer, I need you to come to the staging area. The Counselor is here to see you."

"The Counselor. Why would the Counselor be here to see me?" Luke asked himself. A petite younger lady stood holding a folder near the Counselor's desk next to the guard station. Luke studied her face and body language hoping to gain some insight for the reason for her visit, but he really couldn't pick up on anything. She introduced herself as Counselor Davis. "How are you getting along?" she casually asked him.

Luke really didn't want to look her in the eye or be honest about his current state of mind. He never had been good at communicating his feelings which would have been quickly validated by Stephanie, his wife. "I'm okay, I guess," was the only answer that came to his mind.

"Well, Mr. Berringer, I have received some concerns from our staff in your unit that you might have been discussing wanting to harm yourself. Have you had thoughts of wanting to harm yourself?" She prodded Luke to answer her inquiry.

Immediately, Mike came to Luke's mind. He was the only person he had discussed methods of offing oneself. He quickly came to understand that Mike had ratted him out. Not out of concern for his safety, but most likely to gain a position to help himself. Luke felt disdain and disgust for his roommate. He had never been a violent person but this time he wished he could get his hands on Mike's scrawny little neck.

Denying having any thoughts of suicide would simply result in a trip back to his cell and needing to confront Mike, whom he might just strangle to death at this point. Luke responded, "I guess I have thought about killing myself. The voice in my head tells me it is the best thing for my family. Me being dead and all."

Demetri couldn't believe his demon ears. Why would he say this to her? This will complicate everything!

45

Counselor Davis motioned over to the guard that had been standing just out of hearing range but close enough to react should Luke decide to become aggressive. She spoke to the guard, "I'm going to move Mr. Berringer down to the Special Housing Unit." Looking towards Luke with sympathetic eyes she said, "Would that be good with you Mr. Berringer? It puts you in a place where we can get you some help."

Luke knew there was no better option than to comply with her wishes. He knew he couldn't return to his cellmate. The guard asked Luke to sit down at the Counselor's desk while he made a phone call to Special Housing to get him a cell. Ms. Davis left and a short while later the Guard handcuffed Luke, which was standard procedure, and escorted him out of the unit and into his new housing unit.

"No…no, this is not the means I wanted! Demetri was upset with himself and began to seek a solution that would remedy this blunder. A blunder he had no passes in his present situation to commit.

Chapter 11:
First Visions

A YOUNG ALEX DANTE stood by the casket that contained his father's body. At this early age he had no comprehension of death, and certainly couldn't imagine that the man who was his dad, was now contained in this ornamental mahogany box with gold handles. His mother walked over in her mid-length black dress and placed her hands on her seven-year-old son's shoulders.

He loved his mother. Alex loved his father too, but he had always felt a stronger bond to his mom. He cherished their weekly journey to church and then, after the service, his mother and he would go to lunch at one of their favorite restaurants. It was during these lunches that Alex would discuss the sermon and ask his mother questions about what he had just heard. She was always astonished that Alex paid so much attention to the message. In fact, he truly understood much more than she ever could.

Alex had asked his father why he didn't go to church services with them, but his typical answer was that he was too tired, and Sunday was his day of rest. His father worked a lot. So much that it finally killed him in a freak accident at the paper mill where he worked on the big paper making machine. Now, his dad could rest and not be tired anymore.

Pastor Hammond Oliver, who conducted the funeral services for his father, came over to where Alex and his mother were standing.

"Mister Dante, you, as always, show me a maturity beyond your years. I have no doubt, now that you are the man of the house, you will take good care of your mother."

Alex wasn't exactly sure what Pastor Oliver meant by that statement, but he liked him very much and smiled. The pastor expressed his condolences to Alex and his mother and explained that the pallbearers would be moving the casket to the gravesite to lay his father to eternal rest.

His mother acknowledged her approval to move the funeral services outside. Alex thought the church's cemetery was quite peaceful. Even though his dad never went to church, he was glad they made room for him here because after attending Sunday church service, he could stop and say hello to his dad, before he and his mother went to lunch.

Alex sat down on a chair in the front row next to his mom and she cupped his seven-year-old hand in hers. It bothered him a little that she held his hand with the same hands that held a moist handkerchief. She had blown her nose several times with that same cloth, and it just seemed a little gross to his young brain. He said nothing though and didn't try and remove his hand. It just wouldn't be right, and his mom needed him to comfort her right now.

Directly across from where Alex sat, facing the side of the casket, Pastor Oliver completed his prayer and signaled to have the casket lowered into the hole in the ground that would hold his father. His mother stood and walked to the hole and threw a single rose on top of the casket as it came to rest at the bottom of the grave. The Pastor strode over to where Alex was standing and gently placed his hand on Alex's shoulder while holding his bible in his other hand. Alex looked up at Pastor Oliver who was a relatively tall man and gained his attention.

"Pastor," Alex spoke.

"Yes Alexander," Oliver replied staring down at the boy as if an eagle on a high branch.

"Who are those big men and why are they staring at me?" Alex inquired.

Looking at everything around him, Pastor Oliver returned his gaze to Alex and with a dumbfounded look answered, "Which men, Alexander?"

"Those men across the hole from where my father lies. The men who stare and look scornfully at me," Alex responded as he pointed in the direction of the men he saw.

Pastor Oliver looked up from Alex to take another gaze around the area and again returned his attention to Alex. "My boy, there aren't any men there!"

Chapter 12:
Chance

STEPHANIE BERRINGER WAS NEW to the Christian faith. A girl friend, who had consoled her as she struggled with her marriage to Luke, suggested that she attend services with her at Seaside Community Church. She convinced Stephanie that even though things seemed bleak, Jesus loved her, and was in control.

When the miscarriage happened, it was Pastor Glen and Margaret Firestone that came to her aid and counseled her. Without them, she wasn't sure she would still be alive. Now with Luke in jail, and facing tough charges, she was lost in what she should do.

The local bus route made a stop only a half block from the church. Stephanie didn't have a car and the bus was her only option to get around Seaside. She stepped off the bus and began to walk the short distance to the entrance of the church. The first time she had visited the church her anxiety was the highest she had ever felt. Still, Stephanie knew her life was on a downward spiral, and she gathered the strength to enter. Today felt very much like that first day, except Jesus was with her today. As she walked through the glass doors of the front entrance Stephanie was greeted by Pastor Glen. He embraced her and she welcomed the kindness and comfort it gave her.

"So glad you came today, Stephanie." He held up his left hand pointing toward his office and invited Stephanie to join him there. Once inside his office, Glen asked Stephanie to sit down, and he retreated to the chair next to hers versus sitting behind his desk. Glen was like that. He preferred to be next to somebody as their friend when that person was in crisis. The best therapy he could offer today would most likely be listening.

Before the session began, Glen reached over and took Stephanie's hand in his and said a prayer. She appreciated the prayer because it hit home with everything she was hoping and wanting to solicit an answer from God. Being so new to the faith, she struggled in how to pray. It was timely to have Glen direct the prayer today.

Glen Firestone was no stranger to the story that Stephanie told him. He could relate because he had been there, done that. She recounted the visit to the jail and her conversation with Luke. As the conversation continued, Glen struggled to keep his thoughts in the moment as he continually reverted to his experiences with his own daughter, Cindy.

The battle between flesh and blood and the spirit world of angels and demons was a real one. Glen came to know this in a hard but triumphant way. His daughter had waged that battle herself and had been losing until a helper came into her life. A gifted man that could help her fight her battle. Frankly, after coming to know Alex Dante and his anointing, Glen realized he had never pondered the active existence of evil in the lives and hearts of men. There was a sense of feeling ashamed that he hadn't considered this. He had certainly seen the light and the miracles it provides. Alex Dante had revealed it to him, and he sought to learn as much as he could from Alex.

Glen in the most convincing manner he could, began to refocus on Stephanie and why she was there. It became obvious to Glen that the purpose of her visit was to ask him if he would go and visit Luke. At least Stephanie understood one thing very clearly. Without God, Luke had no future. Neither did their marriage. When Stephanie's discourse ended and Glen was convinced of the fears she had for her husband, a thought came to Glen. With all the things Stephanie had told him, it occurred to him that Luke may be fighting more than just a hardened heart. Just like his daughter, he could be fighting a demon. Glen turned to Stephanie and spoke. "I would be blessed to visit with Luke and attempt to discover where he is in his beliefs. Do you trust me Stephanie?" Glen quizzed.

"Of course, of course I do," she answered earnestly.

"Then, before I visit with Luke, which I will, I would first like to arrange for you to visit with a friend of mine. Someone who I trust with every fiber of my soul." Glen knew it was not the right place, or time, to spring the forces of darkness on such a young Christian. Yet, he knew that if Luke had a demon, Alex would expose it.

"Who is this friend and why do you want me to meet him?" Stephanie asked with curiosity.

Glen looked at her for a moment and pondered how he would best answer her question. "He is a man of God, and he saved my daughter's life," Glen replied.

Chapter 13:
Chess Moves

"THIS HAS GONE ON LONG ENOUGH. I have grown impatient with this subject!" Demetri was clearly irritated with Luke.

Doctor Filek was a board-certified psychiatrist. He sat quietly and stared at Luke, making him extremely uncomfortable. Luke wasn't sure if this was the doctor's method to try and solicit conversation from his patients, but Luke didn't like him at all. It had been a week since Luke had been sent to the Special Housing Unit at the Detention facility and this was the first time he had been seen by any kind of shrink.

"How do the meds we have you taking make you feel?" Doctor Filek quizzed Luke.

"I feel out of it doc. Like I'm disconnected from everything," Luke replied.

Shifting in his chair the doctor peered out over the top of his glasses at Luke. "Tell me what "disconnected" means to you, Luke."

"It's hard to put into words. I dunno…I guess it means alone."

The doctor wrote something on the pad of paper he had on the desk in front of him. "Do you still feel like you want to hurt yourself?" Filek solicited a response.

Luke pondered that question for a moment, then answered, "The voice in my head tells me I still do."

"Then you aren't alone?" The doctor quizzed.

Luke scratched his head and looked up at the white ceiling tiles above him. "No, I guess I am never alone. The voice speaks to me and tells me what my plan is all the time. Almost constantly," Luke answered.

The doctor looked intently at Luke. "Is this one voice or many voices that speak to you?"

"Only one," Luke answered.

Dr. Filek scribbled more notes on the paper. His focus turned back to Luke. "Luke, I believe we can help you much more than we are able to here at the jail. I feel we need to have you moved somewhere that will give you better care."

"*Move?*" Demetri fumed at this suggestion!

Luke responded, with a glimmer of hope, "Where would I go doctor? Would I be released?"

"No, unfortunately not released, Luke. I don't believe you are well enough to be on your own. My goal would be to get you moved to a regular hospital that can care for people, like yourself."

Demetri sensed that, if he were mortal, there would be a certain degree of panic etched on his face. He knew what this idiot human, doctor, was going to say, and it shook him.

"I would like to send you to the Oregon State Hospital. They have a special section that holds patients like yourself. Patients that, you know, are facing criminal charges." He conveniently left the word "*Mental*" out of the hospital name, so as not to alarm Luke.

The words Dr. Filek spoke certainly alarmed Demetri. As quick as they came out of the doctor's mouth, the sense of panic became very real to the demon. The name of a mortal enemy immediately entered his thoughts, "Alex Dante."

Chapter 14:
Union

SITTING ON THE EDGE OF HIS BUNK, Luke opened the white Styrofoam container that held the meager breakfast of one pancake with some liquid resembling maple syrup, a sausage patty, which almost certainly was not made of any real meat, and a juice box. He missed coffee, just as much as he did whiskey. Instant coffee was available to buy as a commissary item but that would require money. Obviously, nobody deemed him worthy enough to deposit any funds on his inmate account for him to use to buy a few pleasures in life.

Demetri thought that if Luke could kill himself with the coffee, he would find a way to get it for him. This subject, and the eventual deliverance of his soul to his master, was spiraling out of control and Demetri was growing impatient. "I must keep my wits about me," he thought trying to reassure himself of this fact. "This is just the type of situation I found myself in with that Firestone girl. No mortal is going to defeat me. This time around. I am much smarter and more powerful." In a subtle way Demetri wondered if another encounter with Alex Dante was what he truly wanted. He would never admit it to himself, but deep down he wasn't sure if his master had truly empowered him enough to challenge Dante this time. Were his powers significantly increased enough to take on this mysterious mortal?

A knock on the door startled Luke. Standing at his cell door was Deputy Peterson, one of the Special Housing Unit guards. He leaned towards the intercom that allowed him to talk into the cell without opening the door. Most of the cells in this area were like that. Luke figured the less they had to expose themselves to the nut jobs inside these cells, the better.

"Hey Berringer, transportation will be here soon. You'll be heading over to the hospital. I have all your belongings packed and ready to go, don't worry."

Luke wasn't worried. His belongings in the jail had been minimal. Mostly hygiene stuff and he was sure he could probably duplicate that stuff at the hospital. Still, Luke felt anxiety about going. He knew what type of hospital it was and to define him as in need of extreme psychiatric care was hard for him to fathom. He felt he was just a drunk, who wanted to die, nothing more.

On the other hand, Demetri's anxiety was intense. After all, this hospital was where he had suffered his one and only defeat, and it was almost devastating. Most of his anxiety was centered on just how he could propel Luke to end his life once they were there at the hospital. He knew repeating the method he used for Cindy Firestone would almost guarantee failure. No, this time it would require cunning and savvy. Something new.

The cell door opened and in walked the transportation guard with wrist and ankle restraints. Luke complied without incident and within minutes he was on his way in a van, to the State Mental Hospital. The distance between the jail and the hospital wasn't far, so Luke took every moment afforded to him to admire the beauty of the Oregon landscape. He missed the river, the fishing, the marine air in his nostrils, yet his thoughts were almost entirely occupied with Stephanie and where she was, and what she was doing right then. He pondered how much it would mean to her if instead, he was enjoying this beautiful landscape with her.

Despite the relative old age of the hospital building, Luke was surprised at just how well it was maintained. As he shuffled from the transport van into the entrance, he was looking forward to having the restraints removed from his wrists and ankles. A medical doctor and nurse interviewed him and discussed the medications that Luke was prescribed. An intake technician took the rest of his information. Luke was impressed at how professional and kind everybody was here. So far it was much different than the jail.

The technician explained to Luke that he would be in this area for maybe six to eight hours, but then he would most likely be moved to a more permanent room. That was unless he became violent, but she smiled at him with a look that indicated that she doubted that would occur. In what was his usual manner of trying to interject humor into difficult situations, Luke asked, "Is there anywhere to get a drink in here?"

The technician laughed as she left him alone on a clean but uncomfortable concrete slab with a flimsy mattress. Despite it not being very comfortable, Luke laid down on the mattress, brought his cupped hands up around the back of his head and, as fatigue captured him, he slept.

Chapter 15:
Good Graces

IN THE CORNER ACROSS THE ROOM, Gayland sat and studied Alex as he worked. Alex thoughtfully transcribed his notes from his completed patient rounds, typing them into the computer, without looking up at the demon.

"Not sure why you are here Gayland? Perhaps you're bored or lonely, and all our residents currently follow Gabriel's God so you are out of luck," Alex sarcastically commented.

"I wasn't sure you detected me sitting here. I thought perhaps you had lost your power to see us," Gayland answered in a calm but hopeful way.

Still not bothering to look up from the computer screen Alex responded, "Oh, I see you, Gayland. You're fortunate I don't banish you down the portal just like I did the others."

Gayland was taken aback by Alex's aggressive comments, to which he had never heard coming from the mouth of this mortal before. Not wanting to tempt fate to see if everything he had come to understand about Alex Dante were true, Gayland shifted in his chair and sported a torturous scowl on his demon face. "Of all the Angels that orbit around you, mortal, it is *I* that do not tread upon your abilities. It is *I* that respects them," Gayland remarked hoping to find favor.

"Hmm, we'll see. So, tell me Gayland, to what do I owe your respectful presence?" Alex asked.

"It is *I*, Gayland, who knows you're expecting a new patient in your ward."

"And why reveal this to me?

"Because you haven't banished me from your orbit, powerful mortal. I wish to stay in your good graces. I don't wish to provoke your wrath."

Bewildered by Gayland's attendance before him, and even more so by the conversation, Alex had no choice but to continue this mysterious discussion through to its end. "So, tell me, what is so important about my new patient that you want to be involved? If you want his soul, Gayland, you have come begging to the wrong mortal."

Gayland smiled in that sinister way that only a fallen angel can, "It's too late for *me* to capture his soul, master Dante. This patient arrives with baggage that we are both all too familiar with. There are greater forces at play here, and perhaps I can assist you."

Immediately Alex knew to *what* and *whom* Gayland was referring.

Chapter 16:
Meeting

SHE SAT IN THE CHURCH PARKING LOT, in a borrowed car, smoking a cigarette. Now that she was no longer pregnant, smoking was a vice she wouldn't give up except to carry a child. Stephanie was uncomfortable about this meeting that Pastor Glen had arranged for her. Whenever she was uncomfortable, she got nervous, and whenever she got nervous, she smoked.

She watched as a small sedan pulled into the parking lot and parked just outside the Church office. A tall, dark-haired man climbed out of the car and glanced around at his surroundings. He saw her in her car and gave a hesitant wave towards her. He turned and walked up the steps and into the church office. Stephanie whispered to herself, "That must be the guy."

Opening her car door, she leaned down and crushed out the ember of her cigarette on the pavement, got out of the car, and walked to the door of the church office. When she entered the office, she saw Pastor Glen having a conversation with the man she had seen. Glen greeted her as she timidly walked towards them.

"Hi Stephanie. I want to introduce you to a very good friend of mine. This is Alex Dante." Alex held out his hand and Stephanie reluctantly extended hers to meet it.

"My pleasure, uhm..."

Glen realizing his lack of formality and manners, apologized and quickly spoke, "My mistake. This is Stephanie Berringer."

"My pleasure Miss Berringer."

Stephanie responded, "You can call me Stephanie."

After exchanging pleasantries, Pastor Glen invited them into his office and excused himself to get the coffee that both indicated as their beverage of choice.

As Alex sipped his coffee, he was reluctant to dive right into conversation about the reason they were there. He sensed Stephanie's apprehension about being there and opening up about her problems with a total stranger. Trying to keep the beginning of the meeting as light as possible, Alex asked general questions regarding how long she knew Pastor Glen and how long she been coming to the church here.

It became apparent to Glen Firestone that arranging this meeting had been unfair to both Alex and Stephanie and he needed to intervene. He had never asked Alex to meet with anybody attending his church before and it was obvious that this was uncomfortable for Alex. "Stephanie, I asked Alex to meet here with us today because I trust him with your privacy and I hope, with the grace and help of our Lord and Savior, Alex can shed some insight into helping you. I apologize if I have made either of you feel uncomfortable."

Alex studied her face the best he could as it was bowed towards the floor. He guessed she was around five foot four and if the world had not been so hard on her, she would be attractive. Her auburn hair was pinned back in a bun and Alex thought she was close to thirty years old.

Stephanie brought her head back up to look into Alex in the eyes. "It's not that I don't trust you Mr. Dante."

Alex let her continue without interruption so as not to distract her thoughts by asking her to be on a first name basis with him.

"I just… it's hard for me to say… I fear you."

Alex was taken aback by her statement. He had never had anybody say something like that to him. "Fear me," Alex exclaimed as if somebody had thrown a playground ball at his head. He looked over at Glen Firestone who had an equally surprised look on his face.

"Yes. It's not that I'm afraid you will hurt me or anything like that. It's just… well, Pastor Glen has told me you have a rare gift, or power, or something. I'm afraid of that power. I'm afraid what that power could reveal about my marriage and my husband," Stephanie offered up to her immediate company.

Alex felt nothing but compassion for her feelings. Up until now, it was only demons that feared him, and the witness he brought against them. This was a new understanding that he had just acquired about his power that mortals could be frightened by it also.

He gingerly reached out his open hands towards her and asked, "Stephanie, maybe the best thing we can accomplish here today would be for me to pray for you. I would like you to let me do that for you, okay?"

She nodded, placed her hands on top of Alex's and bowed her head. Alex began a prayer of thankfulness and praise for The Lord. What happened next brought Glen Firestone to his knees. Alex and Stephanie began to pray the same prayer simultaneously without hesitation and to the same cadence. They prayed like this for almost an hour. There were times that it was inaudible. At times it seemed like a different language.

When Glen sensed that the incredible event unfolding before him seemed almost over, Alex and Stephanie broke into what Glen believed was a conversation with a third participant, while praying together. What he detected between them this time was quite different. They were both carrying on a separate conversation with somebody else, but not with each other. It seemed as if there truly was a third person involved in the conversation as they were both giving different replies to an inaudible voice.

Just when Glen didn't think he could be more confused and amazed, Alex and Stephanie brought their heads to an upright position and popped open their eyes simultaneously. Stephanie had a stream of tears like Multnomah Falls coming down her face, but it was undeniable the smiles they both sported. Stephanie stood and gave Alex a warm embrace.

"My, oh my, haven't we come a long way since our tentative start," Glen looked back and forth at both Stephanie and Alex. "Can you share with me what just happened? It was amazing to witness."

Alex and Stephanie answered in unison, "Annabel. Annabel just happened!"

Chapter 17:
Waiting

SHE POURED A SMALL GLASS OF WINE and sat down on the couch to wait for her husband to come home. When Alex walked through the front door, she sprang to her feet to greet him. Courtney was apprehensive about Alex's meeting at the church with Pastor Glen and another person from the church. She knew this was the first time her husband had been solicited to practice his gift with anybody outside their immediate circle. They were still learning and discovering Alex's abilities and sharing them with the mortal world, just might not be his forte'.

Alex placed his keys on the hook near the front door and accepted his wife's warm embrace. Courtney grabbed his hand and led him to the kitchen where she poured her husband a glass of merlot. Alex took a sip and they retreated to the couch to converse.

'Well, how was the meeting. How did it go?" Courtney asked with all the anticipation that had built up in her.

Still in his scrubs from work, Alex smiled and glanced towards the ceiling as if heaven had become translucent and visible through it. "It was extraordinary, simply extraordinary," Alex replied.

"I so want to hear what happened, but first I must tell you first about a meeting *I* had," Courtney interrupted like an impatient child.

Alex inquired, "Today?"

"No." Courtney explained that her meeting had occurred the other night after he had explained his conversation with George and his revelation from God. As concisely and accurately detailed as she could manage, Courtney told Alex of her meeting with Annabel Perkins. He held every word that was coming out of her mouth with his full attention. Alex sipped his wine and the smile on his face began to grow with every passing minute as Courtney told her story.

"You think I'm crazy, don't you?" Courtney implied.

"Court, I think just the opposite." He went on to tell her the story of just how awkward the meeting with Stephanie Berringer had been. Alex provided her with as much background into Stephanie as he knew himself. He had been stifled and confused about just what Glen expected from him, and how he wanted to use him. After all, just coming out and telling somebody you just met, "oh by the way, I see and speak to Angels and demons, and I have been chosen by God to battle those demons with the help of the Angels," could scare them away.

Courtney laughed.

Then his story shifted to when he and Stephanie prayed together, and God heard their prayer. They prayed to God to bless this friendship and bring faith to Stephanie, that God, through Alex, could resurrect her marriage and help her triumph over evil. Then, God spoke not only to Alex, but to Stephanie also. He explained that her husband Luke, was now in the control of a very powerful demon and Alex knew this demon very well. God had brought Alex to her and very soon Luke and Alex would face Demetri together, but not alone. God brought comfort to Stephanie that Demetri was just a pawn used by Satan to challenge and get to Alex. In Satan's grand scheme, he had known about Alex and his abilities from a young age.

"Wow, that is so incredible," Courtney offered. "But now let me tell you more about Annabel. You should let me tell you what Annabel told me," Courtney implored.

Luke responded, "I have met Annabel."

Looking a little bewildered, Courtney stuttered in her response to Alex, "But...but how? How did you meet Annabel?"

Alex went on to describe how Annabel had intervened during his prayer time with Stephanie, and how she had appeared to both. They heard her story and how she planned to manifest herself at the right time to help in Demetri's ultimate defeat and banishment from earth.

Feeling a little depressed and dejected Courtney spoke in a pouting manner, "I'm not sure then why she came to me the other night in my dream. What would have been her purpose if she planned on appearing to you and Stephanie after all?"

Alex replied to Courtney in a reverent fashion, "To pay the respect to you that you deserve, as my bride."

"She said that?"

"Yep, she said she envies you and is in awe of you for being my choice. She reveres you for the love you give to me and your belief in my purpose and future. Annabel wants you to know she will be there to protect me, *for you.*"

Courtney's eyes welled up with tears, not from sadness but from joy. "I guess we battle those things not of flesh and blood, with Angels *and* ghosts!" She meant that with all due respect.

Alex proceeded to detail his meeting with Gayland, including Gayland's willingness to divulge the second coming of Demetri. "Why can't you just banish that conniving demon and be done with him?" Courtney asked.

"Because he amuses me, and I have other plans for him," Alex confided.

The events of the day had been exhausting to Alex and as much as he wanted to sleep, he also needed to spend time with the love of his life. They continued to sip their wine together and the rest of the evening's conversation was dedicated to small talk. Upon finishing their supper Alex declared he was heading in to take a shower before bedtime. He peeled off the top of his hospital scrubs and headed towards the bathroom. Courtney stood to collect the dishes from the table.

"Do you mind if I save these for later and join you?"

As the water poured over them, they kissed passionately. It would be morning before the dishes were washed.

Chapter 18:
Once

THE IMPACT OF THE MEETING with Pastor Glen and Alex Dante still resonated in Stephanie's mind. It was impossible for her to fathom the events that would undoubtedly change her life forever. The interchange between herself, Alex, and Annabel Perkins was something she could never explain to anyone, including her husband. She scarcely understood it herself.

Things weren't always bad between Luke and her. Having met him when he was their boat guide on a salmon fishing trip to Buoy Nine, where the Pacific Ocean and the mouth of the Columbia River meet. It was an instant attraction. To her, he had all the things she was looking for in a man, rugged looks, a boisterous laugh, and a shyness that comes when a tough guy gets around a pretty girl.

She used to feel pretty, at least from the beginning Luke made her feel that way. Until a of bottle whiskey replaced her in his eyes. Luke was the king of the salmon fishing guides in Astoria. His boat had the reputation as *the* boat to book if you wanted to catch fish. He had that knack. Very rarely was his boat skunked when other boats didn't fare so well. All was good then, and money was pouring in. So much so that Luke was able to buy Stephanie the engagement ring of her dreams. Of course, she would marry him. He was everything she wanted in a man. On a beautiful August afternoon, with family, friends and almost the entire sport fishing industry of Astoria, Oregon in attendance, they were married. It was a beautiful wedding. There was dancing with food galore and the celebration was in full swing. And of course, there was an open bar. Luke felt it was needed because his fellow fishing guides liked to drink.

Stephanie wanted to limit the amount of alcohol that was served at the reception, but Luke thought it would reflect badly on him with his peers if he didn't have the celebration of a lifetime. What Stephanie didn't realize at the time was these celebrations occurred quite often, and for just about any reason. Luke was the king, and he had to convince everybody around him of it, that included himself.

She was tolerant at first believing that it was just the nature of the business. Everybody looked up to her husband, so they deserved his time. Soon, they garnered more of Luke's time than Stephanie was receiving. That's when the problems started. The arguments would peak, then valley, as Luke would stifle his drinking to try and gain some peace with his wife. He truly did love Stephanie, but he also liked being king of the fishermen. His friends could stoke his ego in a way that Stephanie failed.

Luke began to believe that her demands on his business and the drive for wealth far exceeded her pure love for him. He was feeling more and more lonely, and the only way he could battle that loneliness was at the bottom of a bottle of whiskey. Often, he retreated to the boat to sleep, and commune with the bottle. Despite his success as a fishing guide, Luke was only part owner of the boat he captained. In fact, the major financial investment in the boat was primarily with Tidewater Fishing Excursions.

They put up their money to purchase, maintain and outfit the boat, and Luke Berringer was its Captain. Slow but sure Luke began to pay down the debt to his financial partners, but he still had a long way to go to make the boat solely his own.

Many of those nights that he drank himself to sleep he wondered if Stephanie really appreciated the hard work it took to build this business for their future, and for their children. Luke smiled to think what a nice thought having children would be. He knew deep down that he was drinking too much and had recently tried to make amends with Stephanie. The brief reconciliation their marriage experienced had resulted in a pregnancy that would make Luke the father he dreamed of. He was not a religious man so when Stephanie started going to a church in Seaside, he figured they might teach her how to be a better wife.

One day his son, because he must have a son, would be the sole owner and Captain of his own boat that his father had passed to him. He would stop drinking as soon as his baby boy was born, he would stop drinking and become the type of father he needed to be. With that thought Luke rolled over in the makeshift bunk he had made on the boat and passed out. He had no comprehension that when he turned his left arm he knocked the kerosene gas lamp over onto the deck, spilling its contents and the resulting fire would soon engulf the entire vessel.

Stephanie woke from a hard sleep feeling terrified. She didn't know why? Everything was quiet and she looked over to where her husband should be sleeping next to her, but it was empty. Pastor Firestone had offered that the best thing she could do at a time like this was to pray for Luke. She cried as she prayed. The memories she had of falling in love with Luke, and the events that brought her to where she was today, resonated vividly in her mind. Stephanie was grateful to have met Annabel today. Annabel gave her comfort in understanding that a demon was controlling

Luke but had not been with him long. In a way, she wished it could have explained everything that happened before. The same demon who had been with Annabel was now with her husband and somehow, someway, Alex Dante would, once again, expose him and fight to save her husband. "Pastor Glen was right. He was right to push me to meet Alex Dante," Stephanie whispered to herself in earnest hope. She clutched her now empty womb and for the first time in a long time, she had hope.

Chapter 19:
Ghost

LUKE FELT NO COMFORT IN HIS ROOM on ward fifteen at the Astoria Mental Hospital. Albeit it was better than a jail cell, especially one with Prison Mike as a cell mate. This room seemed, Luke struggled for the word, and it finally came to him, *clinical.*

He wasn't quite sure why he felt so nervous or agitated today. He should be happy to have a comfortable bed, a window that let sunlight in, and certainly there were more ways he could end his life here.

Demetri was the reason he was nervous and agitated. A demon that was feeling out of control during a possession could influence its host. Demetri was very aware of his surroundings. To be back at the scene of his only defeat made him feel extremely uncomfortable. "I should have chosen a female. How lazy of me. To be back at this place makes me no better than Gayland."

Alan, the night attendant in ward fifteen opened the door to room number two and stuck his head in as he spoke to the attending law enforcement agent assigned to watch Luke. "Just letting you know that my replacement will be here soon, and he will come in and introduce himself."

"Great," said the officer, and Alan excused himself and pulled the door shut as he left.

Luke shifted in his bed best as he could since he was shackled to the bed by three limbs. Upon hearing that the shift change was coming soon, he felt a little nauseous. He was perplexed as to why this new grunt would cause him to feel this way. Still, the more he dwelled on it the more it bothered him.

A knock on the door came a short time later as a jovial Alex Dante bounded into room number two. The officer on watch lifted his head to greet Alex. "Good morning, my name is Dante, Alex Dante, and I'm the day attendant here. I will be assisting you by answering any questions you might have, getting any hygiene supplies you need, and assisting the nurse and doctors while they attend to you."

"He is no match for me. How unimpressive he is, and I suspect he has lost his power from Gabriel. He does not even see me now and Gabriel had no foresight to believe I would return. Dante is alone, and this weakness will be his downfall," Demetri forced these thoughts as if trying to indwell himself.

The officer exchanged introductions with Alex and then introduced Alex to Luke.

"Pleasure to assist you Mr. Berringer. I trust I will be able to earn your respect," Alex offered.

Luke studied Alex's face after his greeting. It perplexed him as to why he would even want to gain his respect. Hoping to find a way to use Alex as a means to his end he couldn't read Alex. "Thank you, sir," Luke responded having nothing else to offer.

"Sir my foot. He is no Sir!" Demetri laughed in a cynical demon way.

Alex turned to head out of room number two to begin his rounds, but prior to departing he responded with a statement that confused the officer and Luke alike.

"I will speak to you soon, Demetri," as if he were speaking to a ghost.

Chapter 20:
Inquisition

THREE DEMONS STOOD BEFORE THEIR MASTER to deliver the message about the young boy they had spied upon at the gravesite of his father, and all three were certain of the child's ability to see them.

"Did you speak to the child?" Lucifer inquired.

Afraid to answer their master in fear of bringing his scorn upon them, Lucifer asked the demons in a different way. "Perhaps you did not understand my question? What made you feel this young mortal knew you were there?"

One of the demons sensing that their master had lost his patience with them offered up an explanation. "The boy spoke of us to the man of Gabriel's God. The man of the cloth."

"And did the man of the cloth see you?" Lucifer pushed clearly irritated.

The second demon upon seeing the heat fall towards his partner spoke, "The man of the cloth disputed the child's vision of us, so no, He did not see us."

Lucifer stroked his chin as if a long beard existed there and pondered the information his demons had brought to him. After some time, Lucifer turned to the third demon and asked, "You have yet to speak of what you witnessed."

The third demon replied with great caution in his voice, "Master, I do not know of mortals who can see us. If there were such a mortal, especially a child, I believe you would have let us know."

Lucifer continued to stroke his chin in a contemplative manner as he listened to the demon. "You are wise to not have offered this opinion too quickly. I reward my hosts that show patience and wisdom. You have been wise to consider and delay your response."

"Thank you master," replied the third demon.

"Because I am the one that knows everything, I task you, Gayland, to follow this boy from here on out and bring me news of his development."

With that command, Gayland departed from Lucifer.

Chapter 21:
Absence

LUKE AND HIS ATTENDING OFFICER shared the same puzzled look after Alex had left the room.

"Who was he talking to?" the officer quizzed Luke.

Luke responded, "I'm not really sure. Somehow, he got the impression my name is Demetri. Strangest thing I have ever seen or heard. It was like he was looking right through me."

The officer returned his attention to the book he was reading and mumbled something to the effect of, "I will set him straight on what your name is when he comes back. Strange fellow that one is."

"The mortal still possesses the power! He knew I was here but chose to ignore me. He did that on purpose! He did that to deceive me! Yet, why did he acknowledge my presence? He could have used the element of surprise against me had he not tipped his hat." Demetri was becoming more and more confused on who and what Alex Dante was. He knew one thing for sure, and that was that he needed to finish his work here and move on. His intrigue with this human was forcing him to lose his focus and that was something he could not afford to do, not now. Still, he was perplexed as to why Alex Dante was so nonchalant about his presence. It was becoming more and more clear that he must confront this mortal. "After all, I am Demetri, a powerful angel of the true god, Lucifer. He has dispatched me and provided me with the power to take on the challengers of this earthly realm." Demetri had convinced himself that he would not, and could not, continue with the task at hand until he understood just what part this mortal played in his mission. With that acknowledgement, Demetri exited his host and set off to seek his adversary and confront him head on.

As Luke sat in an uncomfortable vinyl chair that he assumed used to be red in color, but now was at best, a color he would define as pink, he noticed his melancholy seemed less suddenly. It was very odd to him that here he was in this place, a place that housed depression and despair, and he could feel this good! He hadn't felt this good in a very long time.

Luke began to laugh. His shallow laugh turned into something that bordered on mild hysteria. The officer who was attending to Luke looked up from his electronic book to gaze upon the spectacle before him.

"What's so funny?" the officer inquired.

Luke eventually calmed down from his episode enough to try and answer the officer. "I was just laughing at the thought that today was the first day in a long time that I feel like I might want to live!

Alex was just leaving Steven Sinclair's room after hearing and enjoying just how difficult Winston Churchill could be with The Queen. Alex often thought Mr. Sinclair should write a book about his escapades with the Queen as the stories always seemed so real and entertaining. Alex began his route to his meager office in ward fifteen when he stopped in his tracks at the sight of Demetri standing in the hall with his Viking arms folded and a stern look on his face. "Why such a stern look today, Demetri?" Alex asked after overcoming the initial shock of seeing the demon standing before him. "Not stern, just puzzled. Puzzled as to why you stalk me. You intrigue me human. I have never experienced a human like you and your mystery captivates me," Demetri answered.

'Well then, if I captivate you so much, perhaps you should join me in my office so I can set you straight on why it is not me that is doing the stalking," Alex smugly replied. Alex strode right by Demetri on the way to his office. Demetri tipped his head in a manner reminiscent of a plane executing a sharp banking motion and followed him into the office.

Chapter 22:
The Visit

SITTING AT THE BATHROOM MIRROR combing the long silky hair that she would eventually braid, Cindy Firestone gazed at her complexion noticing just how smooth her skin was. Her alabaster eyes sparkled with anticipation of her upcoming visit with Tyler. Her visits with Tyler had become much more frequent lately, and she didn't mind at all.

Despite her happiness about Tyler's visit, Cindy felt some anxiety that she couldn't explain. This anxiety she was experiencing was a new feeling. It had only come recently. She thought about telling her doctor about it at her therapy session, but she felt it would pass. It hadn't passed.

Cindy stood up from her makeshift prepping table and bringing each hand down the front of her blouse she pushed on the material to iron away the wrinkles. Satisfied she had done all she could do to prepare for the man she was certain she was falling in love with, she also decided to take Tyler into her confidence about her recent bouts with anxiety.

Her recovery had been remarkable in the eyes of her doctors, and she didn't want to mess that up. Cindy had been having conversations with her lawyers about possibly getting an early release based on her recovery. Realizing it was an uphill battle to get released anytime soon, she prayed daily for the Lord to grant her prayer. The life she had rebelled against so hard was now the life she desired to return to, and to work for her Lord and Savior. Secretly, she also prayed to have a life that included marriage to Tyler.

He gingerly walked into her room in fear he might disturb her, but Tyler McIntyre soon realized he was right on time. "Good morning Cinderoo," which was Tyler's pet name for her. Her beauty always entranced him. To Tyler, she is and will always be, the most beautiful woman he has ever known.

"Tyler, my heart, my soul," Cindy responded as she gave him a hug and kiss on the cheek. Greetings like this made every visit Tyler made to see her worth the trip. Tyler had received approval to take Cindy outside into the courtyard. He knew this was Cindy's favorite place on the hospital grounds and he loved pleasing her. The couple chose a bench near a blooming lilac bush. Partly because it was secluded but mostly for the fragrance of the lilacs.

After sitting down in a cuddling position, Tyler placed his arm across Cindy's shoulders. She gazed into his eyes, and he felt it impossible not to kiss her. This was the first time he had kissed Cindy since he began courting her. It was a short duration show of affection, mainly because Tyler didn't wish to attract any unwanted or unneeded attention from hospital security staff.

Cindy felt like she was in the clouds. To feel Tyler's lips on hers was something she had dreamed about since meeting him. "It's about time," Cindy gushed and added, "I was afraid you wouldn't ever want to kiss me."

"I have been wanting to kiss you from the moment I met you. I also wanted you to know how much I care for you and will always be there for you."

She listened intently as Tyler continued to profess how he loved her even if those weren't the exact words he used.

Then Tyler offered some news that shocked her. "Cindy, your mom and dad have been working behind the scenes with your doctors and those involved with the legal part of your case. I have been helping where I can, in fact I have been filling in at the pulpit for your dad so he can be away working on your case."

"What are you trying to tell me Tyler?" Cindy asked.

"What I'm trying to tell you is that you are going to be released from here sometime in the next thirty days," Tyler answered with jubilee in his voice.

Cindy's eyed welled up and her head fell into Tyler's shoulder. He held her with no consideration or concern about hospital security this time. This woman meant everything to him, and he knew her tears were tears of joy. "You will need to continue outpatient therapy, but you can choose a provider close to home. Of course, home will be with your mom and dad, uhm, Pastor Firestone," Tyler corrected himself.

"Yes, I know the pastor," Cindy chuckled, and Tyler joined her in the irony of his statement. It had been a long time since Cindy had been home. She knew there would be challenges in returning to a past lifestyle, but things were different now, things had changed.

Tyler grasped Cindy's hand and looked at her intently. "I will be able to see you more often. It is my desire, if you are willing, to make the stay with your mom and dad of short duration. I hope soon, you will want to come live with me."

Cindy returned his look and like a priest during the inquisition asked, "So does this mean you are asking me to marry you?"

"Well yes, but not officially. I haven't asked your dad yet," Tyler said sheepishly.

Cindy returned the favor of Tyler's first kiss as affirmation that her answer would most certainly be, yes. This kiss was much longer. When passion had returned to conversation, Cindy felt it was the right time to share with Tyler that she had been experiencing some anxiety attacks, but it had only been lately. "I guess it was just the apprehension about wanting to go home that was making me feel that way," Cindy offered up in explanation.

Tyler gave a puzzled look to Cindy and responded with an inquiry, "You haven't seen or spoken with Alex recently, have you?"

Cindy answered, "Not really, he and Courtney have been on their honeymoon, and I was giving them some space."

"I'm not sure if I should even tell you," Tyler reluctantly replied.

"What?" Cindy asked in an inquisitive but stern manner.

"It's Demetri. He's back here. Alex told me."

The anxiety that Cindy had been feeling reached a new level and now she could understand why.

Chapter 23:
Follow

THE FALLEN ANGEL TRAILED his rival into his office. Demetri, who was used to having a great insight into what the future would hold, had no idea how this interlude would turn out. Ignoring this mortal and pretending they did not share a past would not serve him well. Somehow, he knew this fact as truth. He must gain some insight into why they shared a destiny once again.

When he rounded the corner Alex was already sitting at his meager desk in a relaxed manner. This bothered Demetri. He felt as if there should be some reverence for a mighty angel such as himself. "Demetri, so we meet once again," Alex said as he motioned for Demetri to sit down on a chair across from his desk. This custom of sitting was foreign to him. In his world, an angel either stood, or if he had audience with his master, he bowed. Despite how foreign this custom was to him, Demetri decided there was no harm in his paying respect to this mortal's wishes. After all, he had been vanquished once before by the mysterious powers Alex possessed. "Yes, I will sit as you have offered this courtesy to me. I need to understand you and what you want with me," Demetri responded as a guest visiting a respected friend.

Kevin Wollenweber

Alex gazed at Demetri in a manner indicative of two people from different political parties discussing politics. "I want nothing with you demon. I'm just surprised to see you here again. An old human cliché I recall is you must be a glutton for punishment."

It was Demetri's turn to look bewildered. "I am not a glutton. Angels do not eat food," Demetri replied in a matter-of-fact manner.

"That is an odd statement from an angel such as yourself because Gabriel eats and drinks," Alex answered with a hint of sarcasm.

That struck a bad chord with Demetri who immediately went on the defensive in anticipation that Gabriel might be close by. Alex continued with reassurance, "Relax, angel. If that is what you wish to call yourself. In a fraction of a second, Gabriel could be here ready to challenge you, but we are here having this discussion because I already know why you are here."

"What is it you know about why I am here?" Demetri quizzed Alex.

"You have come here with a new host. With you and I sitting here, talking with each other, I know you have taken a huge risk. I understand that once a demon possesses a mortal human, should they choose to leave that host for any reason, even for just a moment, like needing to get answers to questions regarding how a mortal human has dominion over their powers..."

Demetri rudely interrupted and smugly asked, "If you are so wise to know these things about me, mortal, what risk have I taken with the soul that brought me here?"

Alex smiled like a cat that had just captured a mouse, "The risk that while you were out, your host now belongs to my Lord!"

In a flash, Demetri disappeared.

Chapter 24:
Lure

WHEN STEPHANIE BERRINGER HUNG UP THE PHONE, she rejoiced, knelt, and prayed offering praise to God. The plan, which was orchestrated by Alex Dante, to deliver her husband, Luke, with a clear mind, uninhabited by evil, had gone off like clockwork and she was thankful for the opportunity to witness to him, and share with him, *her* supernatural experience.

The man she had previously visited in jail was a broken man, a man who had succumbed to the darkness of the world. A soul void of love for anything and certainly empty of the love that had been there for her. Now visiting that same broken man, revealed a slight glimmer of light still inside. Stephanie was able to grasp that light and hold on tight, like a bull rider in a rodeo searching for eight seconds.

A young believer herself, she did not feel equipped to be the one to lead her husband to eternal life, but she soon discovered that the Lord can provide the words to the least equipped person at just the perfect time. Luke's heart had overcome its hardened state and he listened intently as his wife described her conversion. The cloud of alcohol and demon possession that had dimmed his vision, his understanding, of why he had chosen this woman to fall in love with, had been removed, and his original feelings were restored.

Luke acknowledged just how much he needed Stephanie and even more so, how much he needed to join her on the journey to know Jesus. In what was a miracle of timing, knowing that she didn't have much time before the demon would return to her husband, she asked him if he wanted to accept Christ as his savior. With the short prayer that followed, Luke became a new creature of God, and Satan and his minions no longer had access to inhabit him. They cried and praised together and agreed that somehow, someway, they would get through this and be reunited to begin a new life together.

Alex knew the deed had been done. His plan to lure Demetri away from Luke and give Stephanie time to bring her husband to salvation had worked. He was certain that just as soon as he informed Demetri of what had happened, his demon rival would fly just as fast as he could to re-indwell his catch. It gave Alex great joy to imagine just how frustrated Demetri would be once he realized his mission had once again been thwarted. The most joy he felt was how God orchestrated Stephanie's participation in this situation. He could only imagine how *she* must feel to have rescued her husband, who had been so completely lost.

This had been a tempestuous day, dealing with a demon the likes of Demetri, but Alex still had a job to do. He was excited to visit Luke, knowing the man he left this morning, to go on a crusade to lure a powerful demon away from him, would now be a different man. Just like his friend, Cindy Firestone. With that thought, he heard a cautious rap on his office door and looked up. Standing there with an infectious smile and beautiful alabaster eyes was indeed, his friend, Cindy.

Alex immediately got up to greet her and was delighted to see she was accompanied by her beau, Tyler

McIntyre. "Guys, come in. Please come in," Alex motioned both into his office. Cindy approached and gave Alex a big hug which he reciprocated. He shook Tyler's outstretched hand and asked his friends to sit down. The conversation began with general pleasantries but quickly turned to Cindy's inquisition. "Is it true Demetri has returned?"

Alex, who had always found it difficult to keep anything from Cindy, disclosed the current state-of-affairs. "It's complicated Cindy."

"Complicated," She replied.

"Truth is, Demetri came in with a psychological eval patient facing charges, just like you."

Cindy scowled a little at Alex's answer. "Drugs, alcohol or both?" Cindy inquired.

"Alcohol," Alex answered.

"Well, one thing you can say about Demetri is *it* sticks to the same plan," Cindy replied.

He went on to explain to Tyler and Cindy that he leveraged Demetri's fascination about his own mortal power against demons, plus his abilities to see and converse with the supernatural world, to lure him out of his current host in order to give time for his wife to reclaim her husband and deliver him to our Lord.

"Were you surprised to see Demetri again?" Tyler questioned.

"I wasn't surprised. I knew he was coming," Alex responded.

"Knew he was coming?" Both Tyler and Cindy responded in unison as a duo in harmonizing song. "How did you know he was coming?" Cindy quizzed with the curiosity that killed the cat.

Alex responded with a seriousness that was not characteristic of his usual confessions that usually contained humor or sarcasm. "Another demon who occupies this hospital told me. His name is Gayland." His friends looked upon Alex with amazement.

Chapter 25:
Deceived

STANDING IN FRONT OF LUKE, Demetri gazed upon him with a degree of anxiety that a demon of his prestige and power should never feel. He was concerned that his sleeping host would reject his attempt to enter again and foil his attempt to manipulate and coerce him into mortal death by his own hand. He knew the only thing that could cause that result was if Luke Berringer had become a follower of Gabriel and Alex's God.

He had been foolish to go in pursuit of Alex Dante, still, there certainly had not been enough time while he was out of this subject to make a choice. "There couldn't have been enough time. He will once again be in my control, and I will not make the same mistake again," Demetri tried to convince himself. Closing his demon eyes, he focused on inserting himself into the soul and essence of Luke Berringer. At first, it all seemed normal. Then it happened. Intense pain in the highest degree of suffering and burning imaginable and Demetri found himself on the hospital floor, laying at the foot of the bed of Luke Berringer, crying out to the voices, the millions of voices that sang in glorious unison.

"Every knee shall bow, and every tongue confess, that Jesus Christ is Lord."

He had been tricked by Alex Dante. He had been fooled by the scope of this mortal's power and his cunning, and now through his own arrogance and lack of faith in his master, he had been defeated again. "Curse be to you mortal! *I* will meet you head on, and you will reveal to me what my master will not!" Demetri reappeared in the room where his nemesis, Alex, conducted his business. He decided to arrive with no pomp or circumstance so as to not alert him. He may be defeated and will most certainly face the wrath of Lucifer, but before he begs for mercy, he will learn who and what this human is. Prior to making himself known to Alex, Demetri caught the sound of a familiar voice that was all too recent and painful. The girl with the alabaster eyes.

"The main reason we came by was to bring you some good news. I am to be released soon and Tyler has asked me to marry him," Cindy gushed.

Alex froze for a moment and then developed a smile as wide as the Grand Canyon. "This is GREAT news! Just the best news ever! What did Glen and Margaret say?"

Mesmerized by her happiness, Demetri could not pull his unseen gaze away from her. Much like his experience with the woman named Annabel, he was captivated by this mortal woman. Perhaps that is how and why he lost her, and it had nothing to do with Alex Dante after all. She reminded him so much of Annabel that he couldn't let her go as he had let Annabel go. He couldn't help but feel something for her but that was a human trait, not one of a glorious angel.

He wondered if he revealed himself to Alex at this moment would Cindy also see him? He had never lost a soul before her, so it was never a question he'd had to ask himself. Demetri decided it was not the best time to get an answer to that question. He had enough to contend with now, and since he had lost a second host to this mortal's trickery, he felt no desire to return to a conversation with his first defeat.

Cindy and Tyler were a bit reluctant to expose the fact that Glen and Margaret knew nothing about Tyler's proposal yet. However, they felt it was best not to keep that secret from Alex. "I can't imagine that Pastor Firestone would not welcome this news, so congratulations to the both of you. I would highly recommend you filling your parents in on this news as soon as possible, Cindy," Alex professed.

Both agreed with Alex's suggestion and discussed their future. All the while Demetri hovered invisible from sight. Then Tyler asked the question that Demetri was curious to hear the answer to himself, "With the demon close at hand, and it having revealed itself to you..."

Alex interrupted Tyler's response, "Actually, Demetri didn't reveal himself to me, I did to him," Alex objected.

Tyler agreed with Alex's analogy. "What now?" Tyler inquired.

Alex answered Tyler's open question by advising him that he wasn't really sure. He knew that by now Demetri had discovered that Luke's soul was lost. "Last time that happened, Demetri was banished to the portal to be dealt with by Gabriel. This time it's on my watch, and I'm waiting for him to return to and manifest himself before me to seek those answers which now haunt and torment him."

"God be with you brother," Tyler responded in earnest.

Cindy and Tyler gave Alex a hug and wished him and Courtney their best. As they began their departure, Cindy had a puzzled look upon her face.

"What's wrong?" Tyler asked.

"I'm not sure. I just have a strange feeling evil is very near to us," Cindy expressed with a concerned look on her face.

"She senses me, but unlike Dante, she has no visual of me. How does he know I was violated by Gabriel at my lake? He wasn't there? Well, there is no Gabriel this time to save him. I must challenge Alex Dante. I have nothing more to lose."

As Cindy and Tyler left the ward, Alex glanced at the clock and noticed his shift was coming to an end. This revelation brought some relief to Alex.

"Now is the time. He is alone and vulnerable," Demetri planned with the cunning of a predator ready to pounce upon his prey.

Just as Alex was signing out of his computer, he glanced up in anticipation of his relief's arrival. Sitting across from Alex's desk was none other than the demon Gayland.

Chapter 26:
Sight

EVEN THOUGH HE WAS ONLY SEVEN YEARS OLD, Alex had a mature mind. He understood complex adult issues and, oddly, preferred the company of adults to other children. Later, when he grew into an adult himself, he began to understand why he enjoyed the time he spent with his mother. She didn't treat him like a child and involved him in discussions that in most cases, would be better left alone for a boy his age.

Life and finances were getting quite difficult for his mother now that his father was gone. He would often try and console her as she sat sobbing, trying to deal with the pressures of being a widow with a young child. Still, never once, did Alex witness his mother saying she regretted having him. At least he didn't have to deal with that issue in his young and complex life. Often, Alex would spend time gazing out upon the neighborhood where he and his mother lived. As he sat on the screened-in porch he would recline in the wood slatted porch swing and strain to lift his young head above the wood table that stood in front of the swing which slightly blocked his view into the street. Alex would gaze at the leaves falling to the ground as they had clung onto the maple trees for as long as fall would let them.

Red was his favorite color although the other fall hues of yellow, orange, and light brown, when they mixed in the swirling wind, all brought him the same degree of pleasure. This was his favorite time of year. Maybe because it earmarked the coming of the fall and winter holidays that meant so much to him. His mother made sure he could be a child when the holidays came around.

He wanted to tell his mother about the three men that had been standing near his father's grave. These men were real, he was certain of it, and he could tell they were conversing with each other about him. This was because one of them kept pointing his way while speaking to the other two. He really wanted to speak to his mother about these men, but the Pastor told him they weren't standing there and to quit being silly plus, the funeral wasn't the right time to do so. He shoved the vision to the side because he had to be the man of the house, and if the Pastor thought that seeing these men were silly, then he must forget about them.

Here he was, alone out on the screened porch, watching the falling leaves, and there stood the three men he saw at the funeral, standing on the sidewalk, staring at him sitting on the porch swing. If this was silly, seeing the same three men again, then why were they here, on his street, on his sidewalk? He was not a child known to be of a silly nature. Alex climbed off the porch swing and gingerly walked to the edge of the porch. Carefully eyeing the men, he stepped down off the deck onto the top step where he called out to the men like long lost friends. "Hey, I remember you guys. You were at my dad's funeral, right?"

The three men in almost timed unison began looking at each other questioning and with astonishment. The tallest of the men wore a black leather jacket that Alex thought was exceptionally keen. Despite Alex calling out a greeting to these men, who once again had made themselves known to Alex, none of them responded back to him. Feeling a bit apprehensive about seeing these men again, Alex decided it would be best if he summoned his mother to speak to these visitors. As Alex turned to climb back up onto the porch, he glanced back towards the men. To Alex's surprise, they were gone, and he was grateful he hadn't called for his mother to witness such foolishness as Pastor Oliver had indicated.

Gayland, and the two other companion demons, knelt in the audience of Lucifer. "Tell me Gayland, what more have you learned about the abilities of this young mortal boy?"

Gayland, careful not to raise his head to meet the eyes of his master replied, "The young mortal can see us lord and tried to engage in conversation with us."

"Does he know *who* or *what* you are?" Lucifer quizzed.

"It appears he does not. He showed no fear of us when he spoke."

Lucifer laughed at Gayland's reply. "Well, he shall come to fear me, dear Gayland."

"Shall we continue to keep watch over the young mortal, master?"

"Yes, this, and only you, will do this task for me Gayland. Find a way to befriend him and gain his trust. You, my clever servant shall follow this boy as he will come to know just who and what you are." Lucifer continued to commission Gayland about keeping a watchful eye on the young Alex Dante. "You shall fail at delivering souls to me, but do not be discouraged," Lucifer exposed to Gayland.

"Fail?" Gayland questioned because this was something no demon could accept.

"Yes, fail. I am commanding this. Because you will be ridiculed by your own kind as being inept, as being lazy, and you shall not allow yourself to come under suspicion by this mortal as he grows to an adult. You will be perceived as a novelty," Lucifer continued to laugh at his plan.

Gayland could not force a smile to his demon face. He attempted to offer acknowledgement of *his* master's vision, but he sensed Lucifer could see right through him. Like the coach of a little league baseball team Lucifer spoke to reassure his player, "You are my most powerful and cunning servant. I trust you will eventually deliver this mortal to me. *His* God's plan will be thwarted, and my dominion over him will be affirmed."

"*You are my* god, and I am grateful to serve you, my lord. But what about Demetri? He is your most powerful and loyal angel."

"Worry not about Demetri. Even though he isn't aware of it, he has failed me before and I will deal with him myself."

Now the smile came easily to Gayland. He couldn't help but smile as he departed to continue being the demon shadow to young Alex Dante. Having the knowledge of a failure by the powerful Demetri was almost as good as being trusted by his master with this assignment. Over the next few years, he kept a watchful eye on Alex as he grew to an adult. He did not appear to him or make himself known as he watched the mortal boy turn into a man. Following Alex through his school years and into college, he began to become slightly bored as he noticed no recognition of his presence by Alex. Often, he would pass by Alex at moments of distraction to try and detect if the mortal would notice him, but there never seemed to be any affirmation that Alex sensed him at all.

Occasionally, Gayland would possess a soul for his master that required very little effort or distraction from his main mission. Lucifer seemed pleased with him just like the cat that brought a prize from the field and dropped it at his master's feet. This encouraged him to continue his surveillance of Alex but there were times he questioned his mission and wondered why his master continued this effort. There was so much more he could be doing to please his lord.

He wondered when and where the time would be right to seek Alex's acknowledgement of his existence. To introduce himself to Alex. His master had instructed him to become a *novelty* to this mortal. To gain his trust and audience. Since he had become the shadow to this human he began to question if Alex still retained the ability to see him? Gayland struggled to find the human words that would frame how he felt. Perhaps Dante, what was the word he was looking for, then it finally came to him... "outgrown" them.

Chapter 27:
The Figure

WITH AN ACCELERATED CLASS LOAD BEHIND HIM, Alex prepared to celebrate his twentieth birthday and his graduation from Western Oregon State University with a bachelor's degree in Psychology. He wasn't quite sure what he was going to do with the degree yet, but he was keeping all his options open. His commitment to his studies and the fact that he had limited all social activity to a minimum, enabled Alex to get to this point in his life a little earlier than most people his age. He was a tall, good-looking man and he certainly garnered the attention of the females around campus, but flaunting his appearance for casual affairs, wasn't Alex's thing.

Despite the time devoted to his studies, he always found time for church and men's bible study. This devotion to his religious practices always perplexed Gayland. He professed not to understand human sexuality, but from his point of view, most of the mortals that he encountered were obsessed by it. He thought that, as humans go, Alex was a fine human specimen and Gayland wondered why, since it would be so easy for him to take up the practice of sex, would he waste his time following Gabriel's God?

Going to fellowship with other believers and learning to have a deeper relationship with Christ was natural to Alex. The memories he had of his mother were engrained in his soul and to abandon his time with the Lord would mean to also abandon his mother. She had died shortly before he started college. He regretted never having shared with her that he had seen the men at his father's grave and then once again at their home. He would have loved to have her share her wisdom on who these men might have been. His mother was everything to him and he missed her dearly. Alex rejoiced in the fact that he would someday see her again in heaven.

Gayland stood outside the church and watched as Alex climbed the concrete steps. He wondered if he could follow him into the building but feared what might happen if he did. Not to mention how it might anger his master even though he was ordered to shadow this mortal. His curiosity to learn about Alex, if he were to follow him into his place of worship, weighed on his mind. As he watched Alex disappear into the building to worship Gabriel's God it began to rain as it often does in Oregon. Standing in the rain didn't bother him as he could not feel the wetness of the drops or the cold they provided. He tilted his demon head to the sky and marveled at the number of singular droplets that fell to the earth, as many as there were of his fellow demons that tarried about this earth in search of prizes for their master. For some unexplained reason, Gayland's thoughts then transferred to Demetri and what his master had said about him several years ago, 'he has failed me before and I will deal with him myself.' How I wish I could be present when that happens," Gayland mumbled to himself with yearning as the rain continued to fall.

Alex closed the door behind him as he entered the church lobby. He was grateful to have reached the inside just before the rain began to fall. He could hear the gutters beginning to release the water that was collecting in them and forcing it out and down the spouts. He knew he was a bit early for bible study but spending time in the rectory alone was something he cherished. It was peaceful and gave him time to relax and prepare.

He glanced out the lobby window at the parking lot just to ensure he was indeed the only one here. Alex was startled to see a large figure of a man in a black leather motorcycle jacket. Looking much like a character from Rebel without a Cause, the man seemed to be enjoying the rain falling directly upon him. In fact, he was looking up into the sky making no effort to run for shelter. "Odd fellow, I wonder if he is here for bible study," Alex whispered as if anybody could hear him. Questioning whether he should exit the lobby and invite the man into the church, Alex stopped for a moment. A strange sensation tingled his skin, and a memory came flooding back to him. There was something familiar about this man, but he couldn't quite place it.

Alex shrugged it off in consideration that this might be a lost soul that was seeking redemption and reached for the push bar that would allow the door to the outside to open. As Alex exited the building, he pulled the hood of his college sweatshirt up over his head in an attempt to keep his jet-black hair dry. The man, the figure, was gone. He shrugged at the sudden disappearance of the figure and wished the unsettled feeling it caused him would go away too.

Chapter 28:
Options

ALEX BRUSHED THE CREASE ON HIS SLACKS as he sat in the black leather chair facing his Advisor's desk at the Student Center of the University. He had worked closely with his advisor Lynn Sterling, over the last months leading up to his Graduation. Most of their sessions were usually about Lynn encouraging Alex to consider doctoral studies to achieve his PhD.

As intriguing as that idea was, the truth was, Alex was out of money to continue his education. His mother had been able to set aside some money at her death. Enough for Alex to get his education without suffering a lifetime of debt but to continue now would make that debt a reality.

He had enlisted Lynn's help in going to plan B, which included a paying internship, or even better, a position that might help him start at the beginning and let him move up the ladder. Maybe even a position that if he proved himself worthy, could pay for some of his tuition if he wanted to go for his doctorate in Psychology.

Lynn walked into the room and smiled at Alex sitting eagerly in the chair across from her desk. She admired just how handsome he was and wished she were 20 years younger. More than his stellar good looks, Lynn admired how hard he worked and that he didn't succumb to the temptations offered by most Universities.

"Mr. Dante, good to see you again," Lynn professed.

"Same to you," Alex responded.

Lynn was holding a small stack of papers and set them down on the desk in front of her. Sitting down herself she folded her hands across the stack of papers. "Congratulations on graduation Alex. You have done very well here and because of that, I believe I have found you a great opportunity. It might not be exactly what you had envisioned but hear me out before you hit the reject button."

Alex laughed at her comment. He was excited to listen to what she had to reveal. Smiling, she handed the papers to Alex. "Oregon State Mental Hospital in Astoria," she exclaimed.

The first thing Alex thought was exactly what Lynn had said. Don't hit the reject button. "Doing what, Lynn?"

"It's right there on the paper. You will start out as a ward attendant. You work directly with the patients, you observe, you chart, you work with the doctors to serve as their right-hand assistant."

"So, I babysit crazy people?" Alex sarcastically asked.

"Well, you get paid to babysit crazy people and they have a tuition reimbursement program as a benefit. Plus, the director of the Hospital is an alumnus. He wants to help you. Or here are some cards of financial assistance people that can help you try and secure a student loan to go for your PhD as plan A", answered Lynn as she handed over the cards.

Later that day Alex began to pack the belongings of his dorm room into plastic totes to cram into his car to begin the journey to Astoria, Oregon to begin his new job as a Mental Health Ward Attendant at The Oregon State Mental Hospital. Traveling to the home which had been provided for him by the benefactor of his new position at the hospital, Alex was less than enthusiastic about his immediate future. As with everything he had confronted in his young life, all he could do was accept what the Lord had provided him, make the best of it, and keep his head up looking for a better opportunity.

He turned up the alleyway that was lined with little one story houses all close together and in a row. Alex looked for the fourth house as he'd been instructed. It had dirty red wood siding with the paint peeling on a green colored front door and a two step, moss ridden porch with a wrought iron railing hanging onto the concrete for dear life. Next to the door was a picture window that did not appear to have been cleaned in this century.

The key was exactly where his landlord said it would be which was under a discolored garden gnome in a small dirt area to the left of the front porch. Looking up towards the roof Alex wondered if he could harvest wild mushrooms from it considering the dense foliage that had formed upon the composite shingles. He inserted the key into the front door and reluctantly turned the knob and pushed open the door. Much to his pleasant surprise the interior did not match the exterior in the least. It certainly was a small floorplan, but it was clean if not updated. Alex realized just how relieved he was and sighed, "Oh, thank you, Lord." Based on the appearance of the exterior, had the interior matched the conditions he saw outside, he might have been very ungrateful to his new boss and had to live in his car.

He turned on the water from the kitchen sink and fortunately it seemed clear. The bedroom furniture was older but functional. He was a man of low standards when it came to living quarters and this place seemed to exceed those standards. It would do for now. Plus, the rent was right.

Alex decided to make do without starting to unpack until tomorrow. He had the weekend to get himself acclimated before starting at the hospital on Monday. He sat down on the couch and a short time later he was prone and sleeping. Outside, Gayland stood looking at the mighty Columbia River as its current carried it majestically along. The moonlight cast enough light to see the faint waves making their journey to the Pacific Ocean. "A mental hospital. This could be a good situation," he thought to himself in quiet affirmation.

Chapter 29
Fury

NOT AT ALL PLEASED TO SEE GAYLAND sitting before him in his meager office in ward fifteen, Alex scolded the demon. "I have no patience, or time for you right now demon. My time to leave here today has come, and I wish to do just that," Alex commented as he continued to pack up his belongings.

"It is not my intention to delay your departure. I am a simple angel and receiving praise and gratitude for telling you about Demetri's arrival here with his current host, well, it brings me pleasure," Gayland gushed.

"Well then, thank you very much Gayland. I'm not sure you should rejoice in Demetri's defeat. His loss is a loss for the team, right?" Alex offered.

"Perhaps, but I am also not a greedy angel. My master will be alright with a soul less, here and there."

"Good night, Gayland. Wherever you go," Alex replied.

"Furious" would not accurately describe how Demetri was feeling right now. Not only had his anger towards Alex Dante increased, but he despised his own demon species, and particularly Gayland, immeasurably more than he had previously. Had Gayland become so lazy and despicable that he had begun abetting the likes of a mortal adversary such as Alex Dante, to the point he would sacrifice and risk his own peace by assisting him in turning souls to Gabriel's God? Demetri had wanted to kill Alex Dante. Now, he wanted Gayland dead also.

His master must know of the debauchery of his worthless servant. He may have just lost a prize for his master, but he never did it in betrayal. Soon, his fellow demon would be placed where only sorrow and torment existed.

Chapter 30:
News

COURTNEY'S APPEARANCE STARTLED ALEX as he walked through the front door and found her curled up in a blanket on the couch and looking as pale as a ghost. "Oh my, are you sick?" Alex said as he rushed to sit down next to her. Courtney replied, "I've been throwing up all day, but I'm feeling a little better now."

Alex sat on the couch and held her. Deeply concerned, he asked if he could get her anything. He was feeling somewhat guilty because he hadn't been home earlier to comfort her.

"I don't need anything. Now that you're home, I feel much better," Courtney replied.

"What do you think this is? A stomach virus or perhaps food poisoning?"

She managed a smile to the best of her ability. "No, my dear husband. I'm pretty sure you did this to me," Courtney offered.

"Me?" Alex answered with a puzzled look on his face.

Despite being entrusted by God to battle the entire demon race; it took a few seconds for the mystery of the moment to sink in for Alex. Cocking his head in a bewildered manner, his eyes displayed the confirmation that Courtney was responding back to him, with her head nodding up and down.

"Oh…Oh my! How… did this happen? Are you sure?" Alex responded.

"Well, if I need to explain to you how this happened then I'm not sure I should let you cook on the stove again! And yes, after the fifth home pregnancy test read positive, and I can't keep any food down, I'm fairly sure."

The balance of their evening was spent sharing in their future and planning for when their family would become three. Her husband may hold the key to the pathway that will bind Satan and his legion, but Courtney marveled at his excitement about becoming a father. At least for the balance of this night, the realm of Angels and demons were far away.

Chapter 31:
Transformation

THE VIDEO VISIT SCREEN CONNECTED, and Stephanie's heart skipped a beat to see her husband, Luke. Over the last few months, she hadn't seen much of him and what she had seen wasn't pleasant. She understood this was a video image and not live, but the transformation was startling. This image was closer to the man she had married.

"Thank you for scheduling this visit, Steph. I know you might not believe me, but I have missed you," Luke said.

Stephanie believed her husband. His voice echoed true remorse. She knew that part of his change was the absence of alcohol but more so she could see that the Holy Spirit now dwelled within him. She couldn't fathom how horrible it must have been, having an agent of darkness dictating your every move. She rejoiced that Luke was finally free of that bondage.

"I have missed you too. I guess what I mean is I have missed *this* you," Stephanie replied.

Luke and Stephanie understood this visit would not be a lengthy one, so they focused the rest of their conversation on making Christ first in their lives. Luke asked, "Hey Steph, do you think you could ask if I can have a bible?"

She responded, "I think you can ask that yourself. I bet they will let you have one."

"Okay, I have never been much for reading the bible but I'm thinking this would be a good time to start." They smiled simultaneously.

The voice on the audio let them both know they had a minute remaining on their visit. Stephanie jumped in with a statement that puzzled Luke. "Your attendant there in the ward, Alex, ask him to get you a bible. Also, if you have any questions about the bible, ask him."

"You know my attendant here?" Luke was startled.

"Yes, he and his wife go to my church. They are very dear friends of mine and I know he will help you in any way he can."

Luke responded, "I'll have to make sure he gets my name right. Earlier he called me Demetri."

Stephanie laughed. She decided that someday she would let her husband know who and what Demetri is, but today wasn't that day.

The swiftness that Demetri rushed towards Gayland with was supersonic. Grabbing him by the collar of his black leather coat, Demetri practically lifted Gayland off the ground despite both demons being of a large stature. Surprised by his appearance and apparent spying on the conversation he had been conducting with Alex, Gayland was unprepared for this action by Demetri. With much fierceness and anger Demetri continued to hold Gayland firmly in his grasp. You are a mortal lover now, Gayland? Plotting against our master so you might go on enjoying this easy existence?" Demetri was so angry that he spewed spittle as he spoke. Gayland attempted to gain his composure despite being in a compromised position. He was able to wiggle out of Demetri's grasp and stumbled backward to regain his balance and face Demetri.

"You are a fine one to speak of betrayal and failure. From what I have seen, you, the great Demetri, have failed in your master's commission once again!"

Demetri angrily quizzed, "And why are you privy to this knowledge of my efforts, traitor?"

Gayland smiled with that *I know something you don't* smile. "All in due time... all in due time," Gayland smirked as if hiding a treasure. That statement bothered Demetri. He sensed that Gayland really did know something to which he was not aware. Then a thought occurred to him, "How is it you are not swallowed by torment, Gayland? You are not presently engaged with a mortal's soul, so how is it you linger here?" Demetri asked.

"I might ask you this same question," Gayland replied with a sense of confidence in his situation. With Gayland's revelation, Demetri began to consider that his time was short. His master must certainly know of his recent failure here and soon he would be banished to facing an eternity of torture and pain. The truth that Gayland presented to Demetri rang true, and his demon body language displayed a defeated being.

Demetri's aggression towards Gayland diminished, "So, you have spoken the truth, which is a task not easy for you, lazy demon. I must admit I am a bit jealous that you seem to be ignored by our master and escape my same fate," Demetri admonished.

"Perhaps you have underestimated me," Gayland replied in a timid fashion. With that statement made by Gayland, Demetri suddenly vanished before his nemesis eyes.

Chapter 32:
Temptation

IN ALL HIS ARROGANCE OF POWER, Lucifer called out for an audience with the God of the Universe. He paced with impatience at being made to wait. He made a promise to himself that once he took his rightful reign as the sovereign of Earth, he would never again have to beg to have audience with the King. "Speak, Satan," God answered.

"I seek your permission to engage one of your mortal servants," Satan petitioned.

"My servant, Alex Dante," God replied knowing *all* things already.

"Yes, he shows protection and blessing bestowed by you. He does not deserve that protection from you, or from your host of Angels. I am convinced that if you will allow me to show you, he will prove to be unworthy," Satan offered. There was a long pause of silence before God replied.

"You have come to me once before with this same proposition and my faithful servant, Job, proved you wrong. This is your nature," God answered.

Satan despised God's answer. He wasn't quite sure what God had planned for this mortal, and it bothered him to not know the answer. Gayland's intelligence had failed

to prove just what God had planned. "I seek the truth about *my* dominion. Since you won't allow me access to your believers, I am here to show you those who need to be exposed."

God laughed at Lucifer's explanation. He knew the answer long before this created abomination thought to ask the question. "My servant Alex *has* been proved. Soon you will know *how* he serves me."

"May I test him?" Satan implored.

"You test all who are my saints, regardless. You may not physically test him but through temptation only. He has the righteousness of my blood in him, but he is still a mortal. Do as you will within my authority, but he will not bear the fruit of the efforts you seek," God spoke. The exchange between Satan and God was over. It had not gone as Satan had hoped and he was becoming ever so suspicious of this mortal, Alex Dante. He decided he might need to confront him himself to explain this mystery.

Chapter 33:
Void

ALEX WOKE TO FIND COURTNEY being cradled by his body. His left arm was draped over her waist and his right arm was numb. He didn't mind. He moved his left hand and placed it on her stomach. He knew it was much too early in her pregnancy to feel anything, but their child was in there. This he knew.

Courtney stretched at his touch. "Saying good morning to the baby?" she asked with grogginess still engulfing her.

"Yep, just wanted to see if *he* wanted to go outside and play catch," Alex smirked.

"Well, *she* says, 'Maybe later'," Courtney chuckled.

Alex climbed from the warmth of their bed to begin to ready himself for the day. "How do you feel? Are you going to try and go to work today?" Alex inquired.

Courtney relayed to him that despite feeling fine right now, she expected her morning sickness would shortly intrude on her current agenda. "I think I will call out sick today. God knows I have enough sick leave to take the rest of my life off."

"Good, I think you should. Are you going to make a doctor's appointment and stuff?" Alex quizzed.

"Yes, 'and stuff'," Courtney laughed.

Despite the euphoria he was feeling from the news that he was going to be a father, at some point during Alex's commute his thoughts transferred to his interactions with Gayland. He certainly appreciated the tip he received from the demon about Demetri's return and arrival, but he couldn't help but shake the eerie feeling that Gayland's intentions were not so innocent.

He was also growing tired of seeing him. Demons were not his first choice for companions. Still, the more he visited with Gayland, the more he seemed familiar, like he had witnessed this demon far before his supposed first encounter at the hospital. Alex shrugged off these thoughts as he entered the parking lot to the hospital.

He was just settling down at his desk to prepare for his day when Cindy Firestone, accompanied by her fiancé Tyler, popped their heads into the office. He was pleasantly surprised to see them and greeted them as such. "I just wanted to stop by and give you a hug and say goodbye. Well, at least goodbye from here," Cindy excitedly exclaimed.

"Goodbye? You mean you're leaving?" Alex replied with a degree of shock.

"We got the news this morning. The judge issued my release. I'll be going to an outpatient rehab center in Seaside. It's Christian based and I'm excited to see what it teaches. I'm gonna be staying with mom and dad until the wedding," Cindy blushed.

"I don't know what to say. Golly, that was fast," Alex was astonished.

He embraced Cindy and Tyler and expressed how happy he was for them. He could only imagine how Glen and Margaret felt. They deserved this peace and this blessing.

"Alex," Cindy said in a way that precluded a statement. "Demetri is no longer here. I don't feel him anymore."

"Nor do I," Alex affirmed her intuition. "My first assignment this morning is to visit with Luke Berringer who was Demetri's last host. I haven't spoken to him since He received the Holy Spirit."

Cindy turned to Tyler and grabbed his hand. "Well, time for us to go and get this show on the road. Please be careful, Alex. I know you have the protection of our Lord, but I still worry about you being in the demon business."

Alex laughed at her statement, kissed her on the cheek and watched them walk out the door. Alex then turned his attention to the job at hand. He grabbed his charts and made his way to pay his first visit of the day to Luke Berringer. He knocked on the door and opened it to find the attending officer engrossed in a digital book and Luke lying on his side watching television. "Hello Luke, how have you been?" Alex asked. He looked around and was relieved to see the room harbored no wayward demon.

"I'm fine," Luke responded as he rolled in his bed to a sitting position.

Alex went over the Ps & Qs of ward fifteen with Luke. Not having any additional questions about how his daily routine would go, Alex advised him that he would be back every thirty minutes to check on him. Just as he was about to depart, Luke stopped him. "I understand you know my wife, Stephanie?"

Alex turned back to Luke and answered, "Yes, I haven't known her long, but she is a good person."

"Yes, she is a good person. Stephanie told me that you know a lot about God," Luke replied

Alex thought carefully about his answer. "Luke, every day I strive to know more. It is my passion."

"She said to ask you if I can get a Bible?"

"I will talk to your doctor. I would guess he won't have a problem with it," Alex responded.

"Can you tell me where to start reading if I do get a Bible?"

"Sure. Start at the beginning," Alex answered. He always felt like he could read people well and Alex felt Luke was sincere in his conversion. He promised Luke he would get back to him with an answer from the doctor as quickly as he could. As Alex continued his departure from Luke's room, the Officer attendant called out to Alex, "Glad you figured out this kid's name ain't Demetri."

Alex could only smile as he continued out the door.

Chapter 34:
Reckoning

DEMETRI KNEW IMMEDIATELY that this appearance at his lake wasn't going to be what he had grown accustomed to. During his latest visit here, he was accompanied by his master, and in fact, the last two visits to the lake had been anything but pleasant. Demetri longed for those days when it was just him, allowed to enjoy the serenity and peace of his lake, without hosting any guests.

Standing at the edge of the tattered and decaying dock he looked out onto the water as it rippled against the reflection of the moonlight. Demetri knew his solitary presence here would be short lived and he was proved correct in that evaluation when a voice from behind him called for his attention.

"You know that each of you that serves me well has their own sanctuary, don't you Demetri?" Lucifer subtly echoed. "None of the angels in my service have a portal that looks just like this. I have often wondered why you chose this lake. It always perplexed me that you settled for something like this, it seems so… so beneath you."

Demetri replied, "Perhaps I am more common than you thought, master."

"Perhaps," Lucifer smugly responded.

"You understand this is a portal Demetri? These portals eventually all lead to the same place. There is only one portal, but each of you chose your own *custom* entry and exit. One way through the gateway brings pain and suffering, the other way allows enjoyment of some reward bestowed upon them by yours truly."

"I know I have been sloppy, my lord. I was followed here by Gabriel and was vanquished. He knew of the portal, and I was not able to resist his power," Demetri lamented. Just as Demetri finished his reply to Lucifer it occurred to him that his arrival at the lake this time was not by the command of Gabriel. The combat between himself and Gayland, at the hospital, was in full session when suddenly he appeared here.

"Then you brought me here, master. Due to my battle with Gayland?" Demetri quizzed.

Lucifer gazed at Demetri in the same manner as a mortal might reprimand one of his pets for bad behavior. "No, I did not bring you here to this place, Demetri," Lucifer responded.

"Well, if not you, and I did not retreat here by my own authority, then who?" Demetri asked.

Lucifer grinned at Demetri as he answered his inquiry, "You were sent here by the mortal!"

Demetri could not comprehend what Lucifer had just told him. It was one thing that this mortal could see and speak with him, but now he was being told that this mortal human also had the power to banish him to his lake, to this abyssal portal! If this were true, then why? Dante had no power here, nor did he have the power to vanquish him. "Why master, why would the mortal bring me here?" Demetri quizzed as trying to connect two puzzle pieces that would never fit.

Lucifer replied in a manner that made Demetri doubt his master's full understanding of the event. "The human believes he has the power to vanquish you Demetri. He believes he is as powerful as the warrior Angel Michael. He believes he is as powerful as me!"

He was even more confused by this revelation, and it was causing him great distress. Demetri had been unnerved ever since Gabriel vanquished him back down the abyssal. He could understand if it had been Michael, an angel that Demetri feared. Michael commanded the army of the Heavenly Host, and he was a fierce and revered Angel.

"But he did not follow me here. The mortal is not here now? If he truly had this power my lord, he would have already banished me to the realm of the underworld. He must have detected that you were present here and became afraid," Demetri lamented.

"Perhaps," Lucifer in hopeful arrogance nodded as he answered.

Demetri studied his master's face. Usually, he didn't stare into Lucifer's eyes when they met physically, like at this moment, in their mortal-like forms. He wanted no, he *needed*, to know what not only Lucifer's intentions were for his future, but also what his master might know about Alex Dante.

"What is to become of me, my lord? I have failed at even the simplest task, the second chance you offered me at redemption."

Lucifer stroked his squared jaw, as he gazed upon his disciple. "I sensed your arrival here at *your* portal. Since it was not me, your god, who summoned you here to this place, I felt that I needed to protect you from the agent that brought you here. I promised you victory when we last met."

Demetri bowed before his master as Lucifer held out his physical hand for his demon to grasp and place his affection upon it. In doing so Demetri, for the first time, was glad human taste was not offered to his kind as he placed his lips on the back of Satan's hand while continuing to bow in a submissive manner.

"Bless you, master, but as I said before, I have failed twice and no longer deserve your favor. I wish to suffer eternal death and beg for your mercy to destroy me."

Lucifer turned from Demetri and walked away from him with his illuminate robes flowing. As he did, he spoke in a benevolent way, "It would well be within my mercy and justification to grant this final request for you Demetri, but I still have need of *your* services. You shall return to continue an audience with Alex Dante. This communion between you and he will be to provoke this obstinate mortal to banish you to this, *your* entrance to the portal, but he will follow you this time and I will confront and deal with him myself."

Demetri looked up at his master with a puzzled look. "How shall I do this lord? How am I to lure one that is protected by the armor of Gabriel? Shall I seek a soul to possess to gain his attention?"

There was thunder in Lucifer's reply. "**No**! I am not quite sure what happened to you Demetri! You were one of my most cunning and resilient servants. Use all your talents and the skills you once so admirably possessed. Seek his attention, his trust, the ugly kindness of his soul, and then use your abilities to turn him against you. He will follow you! He will have had enough of your presence and will want to see to your end! That is, if he truly has *this* power."

Demetri stood, understanding his assignment and its importance to his master. Not needing to be in search of a soul to deliver in order to avoid torment and pain was a luxury he had never known. Except for those few moments he was allowed to be at his lake. He thought just how much the happiness he had known had been defiled lately. It sorrowed him almost as much as when he left Annabel.

Lucifer parted Demetri's company with words that perplexed him with every fiber of his demon spirit. "This is your last chance to redeem yourself Demetri. Since this, your third failure, I have grown impatient with you."

The Keeper

"Third?" Demetri questioned.

Chapter 35:
Turning Point

GAYLAND WAS ANNOYED about his recent encounter with Demetri. It was never easy for him to tolerate the arrogance that Demetri displayed. He kept his opinions close to the vest knowing that, despite Demetri believing he was more powerful than him, Demetri could never hope to have the cleverness that he possessed. Not to mention, the favor of their master.

Knowing that Demetri was probably gone forever due to his abrupt disappearance, managed to bring him some comfort and he could now continue the charade of being Alex Dante's pet demon. He stood in the doorway and watched Alex make his log entries into the computer. He thought twice about disturbing Alex while he was concentrating on his work, especially since Alex had begun to show some impatience and shortness towards him lately, but he just couldn't help himself.

"Your nemesis is gone in case you were wondering. In his rage over his latest failure, I sent him away. He won't disturb you any longer," Gayland falsely boasted.

Alex looked up from his computer to see Gayland standing in the doorway with his demon arms folded and a smug look on his face. Alex responded, "One less demon in my life is a positive thing. I appreciate you letting me know of Demetri's departure. Now please retreat to the poor soul you are now inhabiting so that I may get some work done."

With that command from Alex, Gayland was gone. He shook his head at the empty spot where the demon had been standing and whispered to himself, "Keep weaving your deceit, Gayland. I am on to you. It was *I* that sent Demetri to the portal. It is I that will send you to the same. Lies and deceit are your natural language, and I can interpret your tongue." Alex had enough on his mind and he hoped to have a break from the strain and strife for a while. He knew Demetri would return. He also knew that Demetri, Gayland, and their leader, had all taken the bait.

The phone rang, which startled Alex who had been pondering the upcoming events of the demon world. It was Stephanie Berringer.

"Hello Alex, sorry to bother you at work. I just got off the phone with Luke's public defender. He said that Luke has a court appearance next Tuesday to accept a plea deal to have the charges against him dropped if he pays for the damages to the liquor store and agrees to stay at the hospital until his doctor clears him."

Luke sighed in his response to her. "This is great news. God is great and this must truly be an answer to prayer. Thank you for letting me know."

"I was hoping you would let me tell him. He'll be excited to realize this ordeal is nearing the end. Still, that's not the main reason I wanted to speak to you. I have a question," Stephanie revealed.

"Sure, Stephanie, I'll answer if I can."

"I'm scared, Alex. I know Luke was possessed by a powerful demon and that he was controlling my husband's thoughts and actions. Now he is rid of that demon, through the shed blood of Christ, and he's sober, but he didn't always have that demon controlling him and he still turned to alcohol and away from me. What if he turns from me again?"

Alex listened intently to her question. He thought about his reply knowing he must be deliberate to answer in a way a young believer would understand. "You are correct in your concern, Stephanie. Luke most likely did not have his demon when he turned to alcohol, and away from you. But Luke also didn't have Christ at that time. Without Christ, Satan was able to openly speak to Luke and provide an outlet of sin to lie to him and lead him to believe that *you* were the problem."

He continued, "The demon stumbled upon Luke when he was most vulnerable. Together we must give him the tools to combat Satan. Trust me, nobody hates us more than Satan. Sin is not gone from this world"

"Do you believe he still loves me?" Stephanie asked with the slight bit of fear that she might get a different answer than she desired.

Alex could tell her question to him was in earnest and he decided to answer it in the most honest way he could. "If he loves God, he does. He won't turn completely from sin, none of us can, but if his focus is doing the Lord's will in his life, and marriage, it could be the best times of your young lives." Her smile was not hidden by the fact he couldn't see her face.

Once he had finished his phone conversation with Stephanie, Alex looked up at the clock and realized he was late on making his next set of rounds. Luke Berringer wasn't his first visit to make, but Alex decided he would see him first. He knew he must be careful to not tip off what Stephanie had confided to him, but it concerned him that he would have to be on his guard not to tell him.

Luke was sitting in the same chair he had seen Cindy sit in a hundred times before. It always amazed Alex how alert and pleasant Cindy appeared as soon as her demon had departed her. He noticed that Luke was no exception to this phenomenon. He looked clean, groomed and like he had returned to the world of the living. "Demetri, you sure were hard on these poor folks," Alex thought to himself. He greeted Luke, who returned it with an enthusiasm Alex hadn't witnessed from Luke before. "I have a present for you Luke," Alex said as he handed Luke a black leather New International Version bible. "The doctor said it was fine to go ahead and let you have it. There are several versions to choose from, but this is my favorite."

Luke turned the bible over in his hands several times, admiring it as a child does a new Christmas toy. "I appreciate this, Mr. Dante." Luke said with respectful reverence even though Alex was the same age as his patient. "Happy to get it for you. I see you're up and ready to go to your session with Dr. Lambstead."

Alex walked in a casual manner with Luke as the attending officer followed close behind. As they strolled to the offices where the attending doctors visit with their patients, Luke's demeanor turned to a serious side. "Mr. Dante, my wife might have told you, I prayed with her to ask Jesus to be my Savior. When I was finished praying, I knew it was for real, but I honestly didn't feel different or anything at all. I was just wondering if I should have felt, you know, something?"

Alex wanted to blurt out that he should have felt something different, like maybe that a massive, Viking-like demon had departed from him in anger, but he refrained from any such response. "Most people don't feel anything at all Luke. It's a gradual thing. Still, you mentioned you knew your salvation was real. How did you know that?" Alex quizzed.

"I'm not sure. I just knew. When I was praying, at the time, it was because of Stephanie. I knew how important it was for her and I so want to win her back. I thought this was the way I could do it." Luke answered.

"What changed to make you know it was real and not just to appease your wife?"

Luke stopped in his tracks to look at Alex. He tilted his head slightly in an indication that he was perplexed with Alex's question and his face mimicked such. "Halfway through the prayer, I stopped caring about doing it for her."

Alex recanted, "You stopped doing it for her?"

"Yep, halfway through, I stopped doing it for her and I did it for *me*. I prayed for *me*. Was that selfish of me, Mr. Dante?"

Alex and Luke continued with their slow and steady walk together. It took a few moments for Alex to respond to Luke's last question. "No, I don't think it was selfish of you at all. In fact, this may be the first time you've truly loved your wife. If you don't know God's love, you truly don't know love at all."

"I do love her," Luke added.

"I know you do Luke. I know you do."

Chapter 36:
Tragedy

ALEX WALKED IN THE FRONT DOOR to see Courtney sitting on the couch looking a bit disheveled. He immediately knew her day hadn't gone well from the aspect of keeping any food down. His afternoon with Luke had been beneficial to him because he knew at this moment, he had God's love. It was with God's love alone that he could still love her despite her looking this bad.

Walking over to her and sitting on the couch Alex embraced his bride with all the compassion and patience he could muster. "Rough day my love?" he offered up.

Courtney replied with sobs, "You have no idea!" She was right, he didn't have any idea. How could he? All he could hope for was that she would lean on him to comfort her.

"Is it the morning sickness that's causing all this distress?" He inquired.

Courtney began to sob uncontrollably at his question. When she finally gained enough composure to speak. "Yes, that has been really bad today, but, but..." Then the weeping set in again.

"Court, what's wrong? I need to know," Alex implored.

Her eyes glistening red from crying, looked up at her husband with that look of needing help and rescue. "I'm bleeding!"

In a shocked and desperate cry, he answered her statement.

"Bleeding? What do you mean 'bleeding'?"

"I am just bleeding, and it happens all the time," Courtney responded.

"Did you call the doctor? Please tell me you called the doctor," Alex implored.

"Yes, I called him. He told me to go to the emergency room," she replied.

Alex suspected Courtney was reluctant to go to the emergency room. He respected her opinion on just about everything and never tried to exhort his will upon her. His mother had raised him that way. Forcing demons to succumb to the Lord's will was another matter, but not his bride. She used her common sense in this case to listen to her doctor and within twenty minutes Alex had finished checking Courtney in at the emergency room and she was being moved into an examination area with several nurses gathering her vitals, and all the information they could learn about her. Alex felt hopeless. He took a moment to pray for his wife and unborn child, but he made it quick so as to not lose sight on the happenings inside the examination room.

He understood the medical community doesn't move nearly as fast as he would like them to, but it did provide some comfort to Alex that they didn't feel Courtney's life was in danger. After several hours of patiently waiting for any information about his wife and child, Alex decided to take a much-needed restroom break. He was pleased to see Courtney resting as he left the room knowing how exhausted she must be.

When Alex returned to the room that held his wife, he saw her OB/GYN, doctor, Dr. Madsen, typing some information into the computer. The doctor noticed Alex had come into the room and turned his attention towards Alex.

"Let's step out of the room for a moment, Alex," Dr. Madsen put his arm out as if to direct Alex out of the room. Out in the hallway and outside of earshot from Courtney overhearing their conversation, Dr. Madsen spoke to Alex. "Alex, I am not seeing any good signs from the pregnancy. Courtney's blood work and the ultrasound that was performed would indicate she has miscarried. It was a little too soon in the pregnancy to hear a heartbeat so that is why we depend on the labs and the exam."

Alex was devastated by this news. "Was it anything we did wrong, Doctor Madsen?" Alex asked.

"No, not at all. Nobody knows why these miscarriages happen. The good news is Courtney is very healthy and I see no reason not to continue trying."

"What happens now, doc?" Alex asked.

"Your wife can go home tonight. She is lucky to have you, Alex. She will need every ounce of experience you have to help her through the emotions of this event. I know you are feeling bad also, but I have faith in you to help her heal," Madsen replied. Doctor Madsen went on to explain that since it was so early in the pregnancy, Courtney would most likely pass the fetus naturally, but he would like to see her in a couple of days in his office. "Sometimes it doesn't happen, so we want to check her out to make sure."

Alex was grateful to Doctor Madsen for coming in. He retreated to the family waiting area to gain his strength and composure before returning to Courtney's side. He was going to need all the strength of Gabriel to get through this. He was pleased that there wasn't anybody else occupying the waiting area and he noticed the hospital had provided a coffee pot and condiments for family members. He wasn't sure how long the coffee remaining in the pot had been there, but he was in desperate need of the stimulus it provided. Pouring himself a small Styrofoam cup he sat down in one of the lounge chairs farthest from the entry. There he bowed his head to pray. He thanked God for his wife, and he asked that he heal her through this troubled time. His time spent talking to the Lord gave him comfort and he was able to block out all the activity surrounding him.

Unaware of a figure that had emerged during his prayer, the new occupant of the family lounge purposely came to sit down in the chair directly next to Alex. Upon sitting down, Alex sensed somebody had entered the waiting area. He finished his communion with the Lord and was prepared to exit the lounge area having become perturbed that somebody had decided that sitting so close to him was an appropriate decision. As Alex lifted his head and his eyes adjusted to the brightness of the lounge room, he nearly spilled the coffee he was clutching in his hand. Sitting next to him in all his physical splendor was the demon Demetri.

The demon starred inquisitively at Alex as he sat quietly next to him. He was curious as to why mortals bowed their heads to speak with Gabriel's God when he was absent from their presence. It puzzled him, and he would need to ask this question of Alex Dante, when he got the chance.

Alex stood up to be in a somewhat commanding position over Demetri who felt in no position to challenge Alex's dominance. It was clear by the look on his face that Alex was perturbed by his presence. In a scolding manner Alex addressed Demetri. "I did not summon you demon. You were not invited by me. To have audience with me you must be asked, and I most certainly did not offer that to you tonight. I knew you would return to me, to seek answers for your master, but now is not the place or the time for you to do that!"

"How did you know I would return to you? How were you privy to my conversation with my master?" Demetri quizzed Alex impatiently.

"As I said Demetri, this is not the place or the time. Now please go, and I will call for you later."

Upon hearing the last remnant of the words Alex spoke to him, Demetri found himself standing on his decaying boat dock, alone. More perplexed than ever with the powers this mortal possessed, Demetri sat down on his dock and stared at the moonlight as it caressed the ripples of his lake. This sojourn in which he had found so much tranquility in the past, in an ugly, despicable way revealed the truth for what it was. A lie wrought with deceit. He understood that whatever peace he could extract from it now would be short lived. He must wait to be called by this mortal, and he began to question, whether Alex was mortal after all.

Chapter 37:
Beginning

THE COURTROOM WAS MUCH SMALLER than Stephanie imagined. Her only points of reference were courtroom dramas on television. This court was nothing like that. It consisted of two plain benches offset to the left of the courtroom and two modest desks that sat side by side with black vinyl leather office chairs placed next to them. She assumed they were where the respective defense lawyer and prosecuting attorney sat.

The Judge and his minions were positioned in front of the lawyer's desks, but these courtroom accommodations were of only slightly better quality. Stephanie was convinced this was not the Seaside Superior Courts trial of the century. She had met with Luke's public defender shortly before entering the courtroom. Although she wasn't feeling overly confident in his Lawyer's competence, the attorney felt it should go smooth based on there being a combined agreement on the plea deal.

Luke would receive a reduced charge of criminal mischief on the liquor store damage, and the burglary charges would be dropped with restitution in the amount of the cost of the damage which amounted to three thousand five hundred dollars. The dollar amount brought great despair to Stephanie when she heard it, but Luke's overworked attorney assured her the court would set up a payment plan.

The only other hurdle was if the prosecutor would hold the criminal sentence as time served for the DUI. If those issues fell in Luke's favor, then he would be subject to when, and if, his doctors at the hospital deemed him to no longer be a danger to himself. She sat at the far-right edge of the second-row bench as the conductors of this hearing, including the Judge entered the courtroom. She was nervous until she glimpsed Luke being escorted to his seat next to his lawyer.

He looked thinner than she remembered and the blue suit she provided for him to wear to this hearing looked much too large for him. Still, she had never seen her husband smile at her like he did today. Luke sat down and turned his head towards her and mouthed the words "*I love you*". Before she could return the sentiment, he had turned to face the Judge and the hearing had begun.

Demetri felt no control of his being as he was whisked away from his lake, and his dock, and then appeared before Alex. Somewhat in a stupor about why the mortal had summoned him to this place, his curiosity was paramount in helping him control just how irritated he was at this moment. "Why have you brought me here mortal?" Demetri addressed Alex in a manner reflective of feeling abused.

Standing at the entrance to Courtroom 201 of the Seaside Superior Court Alex watched as Stephanie entered the open double doors to witness what he, and she, hoped was the start of a new life together with her husband. A new life blessed by their Lord and Savior, Jesus Christ. Alex turned towards Demetri and answered. "I know you have many questions about me Demetri. I felt you should see what it is like for mortals, better yet, *believers*, to support each other because of love. Love we received from our

God. Not that you deserve to witness this love, but I also want you for the first time, to see a host, a host you failed to deliver to your master, who triumphed over you because of the power of God's love."

Demetri was perplexed by what Alex was telling him. This demon had no choice but to follow his escort into the courtroom. His curiosity had gotten the better of him. As Alex sat down next to Stephanie, Demetri took his place next to Alex and viewed the proceedings of the hearing. He watched everything intently, including the show of love between his former host and his wife.

Luke Berringer rose to his feet as instructed by the court and listened as the Judge confirmed all the parameters of the plea agreement. When it was over, Luke bowed his head and said a prayer of thanks. As he was escorted out of the courtroom to return to the hospital, he winked at Stephanie to acknowledge to her that soon they would be together and they could begin serving the Lord together, husband and wife.

Stephanie watched as her husband disappeared from her view. She turned and embraced Alex and gave him a kiss on the cheek. "Thank you, my dear friend, and may our Lord bless you," she whispered to Alex as a tear from her eye fell to be tasted on his lips.

Demetri was stunned to find himself back once again at his lake. What he had just witnessed at the court did not make him find peace. It made him angry. It rekindled in him a feeling he had felt once before, and it had been a lifetime before. He no longer felt strong and powerful. In fact, he felt lost and weak. Unlike the soul of Luke Berringer, whom Demetri could tell had hope, he wished *he* could feel.

He looked around his lake, waiting for the arrival of his master, come to berate and quiz him about what had he had just witnessed, like he should have the answers. Lucifer never came. Standing on the dock in front of

Demetri, with all his humanity was none other than Alex Dante.

Chapter 38:
Return

THE DRIVE BACK TO THE OREGON State Mental Hospital was not only one of great joy for Luke Berringer, but it was also a time to reflect and plan. For the first time in a long while he had the desire to make plans. He knew how he fit into *this* future. His immediate thought was that he missed his wife. He missed everything about her, from her laugh, to her spirit, and yes, he desired her.

Romance had never been his forte, but this time he would try harder and hopefully she would notice a difference in him. Stephanie certainly deserved it and, now that he was beginning to experience Christ's love, perhaps he could channel that love into his marriage.

He knew his boat was gone and with it so was his chance to be king of the fishing boat captains. Luke was unsure if his partners would also go after him for financial restitution, but he determined there was nothing he could accomplish by worrying. What he did know is he could find fish and he knew how to catch them. Because of that he would be of value to some boat, and he would rebuild his reputation.

First, he had to get his doctors to believe he could be a functioning member of society again without a penchant for self-destruction. His mind was clear now and with every passing day his desire for alcohol was subsiding. Luke knew that was his first priority, to convince his doctors, because without doing just that he could never achieve any of his dreams.

As he exited the transport van, he was greeted by two staff members to escort him to dress-out in order to change back into his hospital uniform. The uniforms patients wore were more comfortable than the blue suit he had worn to court, so he obliged them to change without objection.

As he was being escorted down the hall, he found it oddly different from earlier that same morning.

This hallway was different, brighter, and much longer. Luke thought about asking one of his escorts if this was a different way to ward fifteen and his room in the criminal wing, but he assumed they wouldn't tell him anyway. There always seemed to be a safety and security concern when it came to transporting an inmate/patient in this facility. He knew he wouldn't see Alex this afternoon because he had attended his hearing at court. Luke had never known a man like Alex. The fact that he was there at court to support him, and Stephanie, was slightly overwhelming. His thoughts came to the realization that if Christian men were like Alex, well then, that is the type of man he also wanted to be. As he turned the corner with his escorts, he viewed the sign above him which read:

Ward 21
Rooms 1-16

Luke had to think for a minute. He was certain his room was in ward fifteen. The escorts stopped at room thirteen and pushed open the door as they directed Luke to enter. He gingerly walked past the escorts and into his room. The perplexed look on his face triggered one of the staff escorts to speak up.

"Yes, this is your *new* room, Berringer. Your criminal charges were dismissed, thus, you're not in the criminal ward anymore. This is a patient ward, and that's what you are."

He had nothing against the officers that had watched him and shared his room, but they were gone now. It finally made sense to him now because when he returned from court, it was sans handcuffs. He breathed a sigh of relief with the understanding he would sleep in this room tonight, unshackled and alone.

The staff attendants walked Luke around the room pointing out the lay of the land. He was shown how to ring for a nurse or attendant if he needed anything or had any questions. After they left, Luke sat down on the bed. It was full size and had a comforter which maybe wasn't made of down feathers, but it was clean and fresh and comfortable. There was a knock on the door and a new attendant filed in carrying a tray with the evening meal on it. He introduced himself as Glen Petry.

"Hello Luke. I'll be your night attendant here on this ward. I will make sure you get to all your therapy sessions along with your doctor appointments. Your day attendant will be my partner, Jim Dubose. You'll meet him in the morning."

Luke nodded his head as he sat down at the desk which had a lamp and a phone. He uncovered the tray and was delighted to find the food was still hot. He began to consume the hamburger steak with brown gravy as quickly as he could shove it into his mouth. It had been a good deal of time since he had last eaten. With a full mouth he stuck up a hand with his index finger extended to get Glen's attention. "What about Alex? Will I still get to see him?" Luke inquired.

Glen replied as he exited the room, "You mean Alex the *whisperer*! You won't get to see him all the time but you folks that come from ward fifteen sure do get attached to that guy. He'll be by to see you as often as he can, you can bet on that!"

Luke tasted the mashed potatoes and chuckled to himself. "I guess they aren't too concerned with me killing myself anymore. The cord from the lamp or the phone cord in here would be more than adequate to do the job."

Chapter 39:
Lake

THIS BOAT DOCK WAS VERY OLD, but for some reason, Alex could almost understand Demetri's affection for this lake and its surroundings. He was amazed that any mortal human, like himself, frequented this area for entertainment and pleasure not knowing that within the confines of the water existed a supernatural pathway to another lake. The lake of fire and the pit of hell.

Alex's eyes returned to focus on Demetri who had directed a scornful gaze towards Alex. "How dare you defile my sanctuary, human," Demetri called out to Alex not fully believing this being was human. He was on the defensive and he believed pushing back at Alex was the only mechanism currently at his disposal.

Alex spoke with considerable calm despite experiencing this sudden burst of wrath from Demetri. "First *demon*, this is not *your* sanctuary. This lake, in all its splendor belongs to *my* Lord. He is the one who created it! I must compliment you though that your only claim to this place is that it is a serene place to manifest the portal for you to return to where you belong."

"Ha!" Demetri snorted like a human cannonball being shot from a cannon! "I guess we'll have to agree to disagree on who is master of this place."

Alex's demeanor with Demetri must have calmed the demon as his anger began to diminish. Partly because he had grown afraid of Alex based on this being the first time, he had followed him to the lake, but also because he had grown skeptical that Lucifer had truly endowed him to fight this mortal.

Demetri decided he must return to the cunning instincts he once possessed but seemed to have forgotten. Alex was like nothing he had ever encountered before, and he must use his demon intellect to try and gain power over him. "So just why have you sent me here to this Lake, Dante?" Demetri quizzed Alex. He extended his hand as he slowly spun to point out the splendor of the lake. "You are obviously wise, and we agree that this place harbors a beauty that both of us can share. If you've sent me here and followed me just to banish me down the abyssal, it seems like such a shame. Might we two coexist?"

Alex laughed as he said, "Soon enough, demon. But I won't be the one to banish you back down the abyssal."

"Who then?" Demetri was puzzled.

Alex said nothing. This captured the ire of Demetri. His anger got the best of him. Then his cunning and deceit kicked in and he bellowed at Alex, "Your child, the one my master snatched from your precious woman's womb, it was a male. Your heir now belongs to that same realm you threaten against me. Perhaps, you need *me* to represent *you* with *my* master? Plea for his grace upon you to be reunited with your son?"

Alex scowled at Demetri as he practiced every degree of restraint he could muster. "I need nothing from you, vile demon. Do not offer me temptation. I am sustained in my grief with the truth and knowledge that my child, son, or daughter, stands beside the God of the universe and, yes, I will see my child again, but not standing with *your* master."

Demetri replied in a spiteful way, "Believe what you must, weak human. Perhaps I can convince your bride to take my offer. A mother's grief can be so much more. All she would be required to do is denoun…"

Demetri found his mouth bound. He could not speak. It was as if duct tape had been wound around his head sealing his mouth shut, but there was no physical barrier present.

Alex could see the fear in Demetri's demon eyes as he struggled with the limitations that he now fought. Despite the lack of speech inflicting him, Demetri began to suffer excruciating pain in every joint of his body. As quickly as it had started, it ended, and he once again gained focus on Alex.

Alex spoke clearly and slowly just before he left Demetri standing on the dock alone. "To answer your question, demon, I followed you here, to this lake and your portal, because I *am* mortal, I *am* human, and I *can!*"

Chapter 40: Feeling

ALEX NEEDED TO BE WITH COURTNEY. He felt for the first time since he had become aware of his anointing from God, guilty. Guilty for running off to put demons in their place. The foul words that Demetri spoke to him, and the threats made towards his wife only helped to fuel his guilt. They were words of deceit and hate but Alex knew from where they had been generated. God had provided to him that knowledge and armor.

He was worried about Courtney and what she must be going through. She had never seen Demetri and that wasn't her gift, but he couldn't help but be bothered by the ugliness of the threats the demon spoke. Alex decided that despite how much work he had yet to do, not only at the hospital but also battling the forces of darkness, he was going to take the next couple of days off. He was going to be there for, and with, Courtney. He needed to be with her for the appointment with Dr. Madsen, and he was sure God would understand she must be a top priority for him right now.

Their cottage was dark when Alex walked in the front door. Although he could now transport between places in an instant, while following demons, his abilities did not extend to his earthly world. Secretly, he wished he could. The time it took for him to get to his home and be with Courtney was one of those moments. When his eyes adjusted to the darkness around him, he found Courtney on the couch crying. He moved over to her and without needing to say a word, his heart ached to see her in such despair. "I have not been fair to you, my Love. I should have been here with you instead of chasing Demetri," Alex lamented.

Between sobs Courtney looked up into Alex eyes. It was not a look of scorn as he had become so accustomed to today, but a look of forgiveness and love. Alex held his wife close and promised her that he was not going anywhere. He would be with her for however long it might take to help absorb her pain and hurt.

Courtney spoke very softly, "I must tell you; this is why I am crying. I am confused and my anxiety is far beyond anything I have experienced."

"Confused? Why are you confused? Please tell me," Alex implored.

"I'm confused because of this feeling, oh never mind, I can't articulate it."

"What? Do your best to tell me," Alex begged.

Courtney looked deep into Alex's eyes. Her stare pierced directly into his soul. Alex had felt many unusual sensations lately but this one was beyond comprehension. "It's just, I feel as though I'm still pregnant. Like the baby is still there."

Luke wasn't sure how to reply to her revelation. He could only stare at Courtney and try to come up with the most sensitive response he could manage. "Is that a normal feeling, like, you know, after a miscarriage?"

"I'm not sure. I can't deny the feeling and the bleeding has totally stopped. I just feel like she is still there," Courtney answered in a bewildered fashion.

"She?" Alex questioned.

"Yes, she," Courtney answered.

Alex suddenly felt invigorated by her revelation, and he immediately led them both into prayer. If this was true, they needed to pray for it. If it wasn't true, they needed to know it was God who directed the outcome and accept it.

He was extremely glad they would only have to wait a day until her appointment with Dr. Madsen. He divulged to Courtney that he would be with her tomorrow at her appointment. He wouldn't leave her side. Courtney threw her arms around his neck and kissed him out of gratitude. Little did she know there was no way he could work and concentrate being apart from her, because next to becoming a believer, she was the best thing that ever came into his life.

Friday came too slowly, and Alex and Courtney sat in the examination room at Doctor Madsen's clinic. After the exam, the doctor had ordered an ultrasound telling the couple that this was normal procedure. This was all new to them and helped to inspire the tension they both felt. Courtney had explained her feeling and intuition to the doctor, but he wouldn't confirm or deny these things could happen. Alex intently studied the face of the ultrasound technician hoping it would divulge any findings. Her poker face was impressive in that he gathered no tip-off that was conclusive.

As they sat and stared at each other Alex smiled at Courtney and she returned the gesture. The tension was extreme as they waited for the door to open and see the doctor coming in to reveal the results of the exam. When the door finally opened it was as if you had just opened a soda bottle and the pressure began to be released from the carbonization.

Doctor Madsen would never be accused of having a superior bedside manner, but in his field of OB/GYN, he was considered one of the finest on the Oregon coast. He rolled the exam chair up next to the computer and clicked the computer mouse to illuminate photos on the screen. Turning the screen towards Alex and Courtney he changed one of the photos to full screen. "Well Courtney, your motherly instincts were correct! Meet baby Dante. This was not a miscarriage despite what the labs and exam at the hospital indicated. I've read about a pregnancy being viable despite what we saw the other night, but I've never seen one myself, until now.

Alex and Courtney embraced. They both knew why this had happened. It was a miracle. The doctor confirmed they were back on track with a normal pregnancy as everything looked good. He suggested that Courtney should remain at rest as much as possible and that should include her not working. He scheduled a follow up appointment in a month and bid them both a happy goodbye.

Alex had to take a moment after placing Courtney in the passenger seat to bow his head and thank Jesus for this miracle. He finished his quick prayer of thanksgiving and climbed in the driver side and started the engine. Courtney was crying in the seat next to him, but this time it was a different kind of tear. He reached over and held her hand and she reciprocated. The sun was out today, and Alex slid on his aviator sunglasses to begin their journey home. He whispered under his breath, "Well, well, Demetri, you lose once again, and soon, for the last time."

Chapter 41:
Barley

FOR SEVERAL YEARS, Gayland had been Alex Dante's shadow. He had mirrored his every move as he watched him grow up in his mortal world. Traveling amongst the earthly constraints of that world was easy for him and he could manifest himself wherever and whenever it served a purpose for his mission. A demon's movements had never been restricted on earth. He was an angel and being spirit, he was never confined to the realm of the physical world. Until now.

He had lost the ability to track and manifest himself to Alex Dante. Gayland was too fearful to confront Lucifer with this predicament. He had never had this problem before, so why now. All he knew is when he tried to find Alex, it led him here, to *his* sanctuary, but Alex Dante was not here. Not that Gayland found going to his sanctuary a bad thing. He wasn't sure where other demons chose to retreat to, but this was his. A white time-worn, farmhouse with a wrap-around porch and a split-rail fence as far as the eye could see. He was never quite sure what crops had been planted here at his farm, and he never cared. He would retreat to his farm, sit on the porch in an old wood rocking chair and wish he could drink the iced tea sitting on the table next to him. He longed to be mortal, just once, and taste that tea and feel the ice in his demon mouth and the that cool liquid sliding down his demon throat. He could almost imagine it, despite the limitations of the realm in which he existed. It was difficult for him to not be a little bit jealous of mortals for that very reason. He often wondered if any of his fellow angels had these same thoughts and let their desires travel to earthly pleasures. Reality drew him back in and he again questioned why every time he tried to conjure an audience with Alex Dante, he would arrive at this very destination. He could not make sense of any of this.

As much as Gayland wished to stay, rocking on his porch dreaming of iced tea, he transported himself back to the hospital. It is here he must wait and be patient, like a mouse trap with a piece of cheese, for Alex to arrive. Perhaps then he would be able to extract the mysteries of his current binding and get on with the discovery of the unusual powers of this mortal and his connection to Gabriel's God. These were answers he must find out or face the wrath of his master. Fortunately for Gayland, his wait would be short. Demons really have no concept of time, but he sensed by earthly standards that he had only been waiting for two of Alex's days.

Gayland sighted Alex coming onto ward fifteen and despite being worried that he might be rebuked and cast away, he stood before Alex. "I was concerned about your absence. I've seen no sign of your mate either and felt as if something might be wrong. You're the only connection I have to this physical realm and if I may be so blunt, without that connection my existence here would be far less, shall we say, intriguing."

Not wanting to wear out a tenuous welcome, Gayland bowed his head to Alex and began a slow exit from his presence. Now that Alex was back, and Gayland could at least speak with him he didn't want to jeopardize these infrequent meetings. Somehow, he would have to get Alex to have the patience to speak with him and to divulge what these angelic abilities were meant for.

Gayland was a bit taken aback when Alex responded to his greeting. "Perhaps I have been a bit too abrupt with you lately, Gayland. The intricacies of being human have been challenging of late, to say the least. I know that's hard for a demon like you, who lives the carefree life, to understand."

The demon forgave the evidence of sarcasm in Alex's words knowing that no mortal could truly understand Gayland's world just because he was able to move like an angel of Lucifer. To show humility and respect to his mortal subject, Gayland carefully gauged his reply. "And I could not begin to understand the strife of human life. Particularly the life of one such as yourself. A human that can see and converse with a being such as myself. Are there other mortals like you? I have never encountered one, if there are others like you?" He knew he had just taken a huge chance with that reply. This human was smart and probably knew what he was up to and was lying.

Alex nonchalantly replied, "I haven't really thought much about it." Which Alex knew was also a bit of a stretch on the truth. "I need to go to work, Gayland. We can chat more later."

"*Chat*," Gayland thought. "How flippant is that remark." Gayland adjusted his black leather jacket around his broad demon shoulders and began his departure. Just before he apparated, Alex called out to him, "It was barley."

"Barley?" a puzzled Gayland called back to Alex.

"The crop they grew on your farm," Alex replied.

Chapter 42:
Reunion

BRUSHING HIS TEETH, Luke Berringer stared at the man he was becoming in the mirror. He had looked at himself before, even recently, and didn't like what he saw. This time though, he was beginning to recognize the man he was before the ravages of alcohol.

Oddly enough, his mind began to return to the water. Once again, he was curious about what time of year this was, and when the salmon runs that come and go with the seasons would be ending or starting. He would ask the doctor if it was alright for Stephanie to bring some fishing magazines when she was allowed to visit. That wasn't the only question on his mind today for his visit with the doctor. When might he be able to hold his wife in his arms and feel her body next to his? Now that the man in the mirror looked more like the man she married, perhaps she would want him to hold her.

"Time to go see the doctor, Luke," his attendant, Jim Dubose, exclaimed.

"Good, good, I've been wanting to speak with him," Luke replied.

Conversation was not easy between Jim and Luke as they walked towards the doctor's wing. Luke missed his talks with Alex. Heck, he just missed Alex. They could discuss the Bible or the best jig to use when fishing for river salmon. Alex just had that way about him and could keep up with Luke's passions. It wasn't that Jim wasn't attentive, or a nice guy, he just wasn't Alex.

Stopping at the office of Doctor C. Ruiz, Jim opened the door and guided Luke into the waiting area. A petite attendant sitting in a small adjacent room to a short hallway greeted Luke and advised him that Doctor Ruiz was ready for him and go ahead into room number one, on the left in the short hallway.

Luke sat in the comfortable brown leather chair next to the more stoic and formal chair next to it. There was a simple coffee table in front of both chairs. On the coffee table were strategically placed copies of Modern Healing magazine. He picked up the top magazine of the group. The cover revealed how yoga and a vegan diet had saved some Hollywood actress's life. He didn't recognize the actress but to say that he had been out of the Hollywood movie scene for quite a while wouldn't be a stretch.

Doctor Ruiz tapped lightly on the door before entering the room. She held out her hand and Luke shook it. She was friendly and pleasant, and Luke felt comfortable with her despite being somewhat surprised his doctor was a woman. He wasn't bothered that she was *his* doctor, he had just expected a male in the most stereotypical fashion possible. She didn't push hard at all with the normal rhetoric such as, did you hate your mother? Did you hate your father? She took her time with Luke, and he appreciated that. It seemed as if she wanted to get to know him, to know *him* personally. After approximately thirty minutes, Luke was comfortable enough to ask his doctor if he might be able to have Stephanie visit.

"Luke, I'm going to be honest with you. You are here to be evaluated to see if you are any longer a danger to yourself. My evaluation, in the short time we have talked today, is that you are not. I'm going to recommend that you attend an outpatient alcohol program, or you will face the risk of falling back into that cycle. So based on that, I don't see you being a patient at this hospital much longer."

With those words Luke realized he would be reunited with Stephanie very soon. The tears streaming down his face explained to Doctor Ruiz that this was a man who had begun the changes to make his life better. Luke thanked his doctor for their time together and he asked if he would see her again. "Maybe at the beach digging for clams," Dr. Ruiz laughed.

Luke couldn't wait to get back to his room and call Stephanie to tell her the news of his visit with Doctor Ruiz. He picked up the phone and dialed the number of the mobile phone that his father had provided for her so Luke could call his wife as often as possible. Luke's father encouraged the communication, knowing just how important she was to his son's recovery and future. Luke hung up the phone after several rings with no answer. A look of concern was etched on his face.

Chapter 43:
Destroyer

THERE WAS A SPRING IN HER STEP. For the first time Stephanie had woken with hope. She was excited to be going to see her *new* husband. She laughed to herself about thinking of him as was her *new* husband. But after all, this Luke Berringer was truly a new man. Christ had made him that way. She was eager to start a new relationship with this Luke. One where neither he, nor she, would lead. Only Christ.

Her father-in-law was trying to raise the money to get the truck he had lent to his lost son out of impound so that she would have transportation. Unfortunately, those fines were significant, and he would require some time to accomplish the feat. Stephanie didn't mind taking the bus. It was relatively convenient for her, and it stopped right at the entrance to the Mental Hospital. "I guess most of the people who are self-admitting don't have cars, so having a bus stop right in front of the hospital, makes sense," she shrugged as she pondered this fact.

Clouds rolled in and out as was normal for the coast of Oregon. Luckily these clouds were not carrying any rain. As Stephanie arrived at the bus stop, she was amused that many of the people who were already there waiting the arrival of the bus to carry them off to their various destinations were adorned in heavy rain gear. Many of the passengers were elderly. "They wear rain gear even when the sun is shining with no chance of rain in the forecast," she smiled as she thought, finding their attire humorous.

This stop was a popular and busy one. It was not unusual to find several people waiting when Stephanie arrived. There was a wrought iron mesh bench that was placed beneath a metal covering with a plexiglass roof that gave protection from the frequent rain. The protection it provided was minimal as the ocean wind could blow rain sideways as the gales of winter would gust and direct them that way. Today was no different and despite the relatively low chance for rain, the bench was full. Stephanie didn't mind standing because most of the riders were older and needed to sit. Nothing was going to damper the joy she felt today. An older man, being a gentleman, offered his seat to Stephanie but she was courteous in declining his offer.

She stood to the side of the overhang cover. Normally she would have lit up a cigarette knowing the bus was still several minutes from arriving, but she was trying to quit smoking. She had prayed for Jesus to remove that crutch from her. She wanted Luke and herself to start their new lives together without any past crutches.

Many of the older folks that had been sitting on the bench stood suddenly and started frantically pointing in the direction where Stephanie was standing. In a manner similar to ants scattering when their anthill is being attacked, the patrons of the bus service moved as quickly as they could to get away from where they had been sitting on the bench. It seemed like slow motion as Stephanie glanced at the former bench occupants and saw terror etched on the faces. She thought it odd that many had left their purses, packages, and prized possessions. By the time she turned her head towards the direction that had brought these actions from her fellow bus riders, she was left with no chance to react. Stephanie could see the eyes of the older man who was behind the wheel of the 2006 Cadillac. Those eyes showed fear and terror.

She stood before Jesus. He was more magnificent than she could ever have imagined. There was nothing on Earth that could possibly compare to God. He was spirit, void of the physical form to which they painted his human likeness. But she knew him, and he knew her. There was no pain, no sorrow, only joy. Those that had gone before her came to greet her as she came to her heavenly home. She recognized each of them. Stephanie recognized Annabel Perkins. They embraced and rejoiced. A heavenly companion reached out to grasp her hand and she knew him. There were no tears, only praise for God. It was her son; she had held him within her womb.

Chapter 44:
Unknown

THE PHONE RANG IN ALEX'S OFFICE just seconds after Gayland departed from him. He knew his parting words to the demon must have confounded his understanding of the normal order of things in his demon world. Or at least what Gayland thought was normal.

Alex picked up the phone and answered. "Dante, ward fifteen." On the other end of the phone line was Jim Dubose.

"Hey Alex, this is Jim. I am hoping you can break away from your ward and come over here to see Luke Berringer. He is asking for you personally and he's quite agitated. I've tried to get him to tell me what's bothering him, but he insists on seeing you."

Alex responded, "Sure, Jim. Give me a couple of minutes to finish some stuff here and I'll be right over." Jim hung up the phone and returned to his patient to let him know Alex was on his way. As Alex made his way towards Luke Berringer he passed by the cafeteria and guest dining area which was the usual route you would take to reach the ward where Luke was housed. Standing off to the side, near the doors to the kitchen area he glimpsed Gayland standing in his usual spot. Despite being in a hurry, he couldn't resist grabbing a plastic soda glass and filling it with ice. Stepping up to the soda dispenser, Alex filled it to the top with sweet tea which came already brewed and dispensed from the machine. He gulped down just about half the refreshing liquid and set the half that remained in the glass down on the table close by the drink dispenser.

He turned and departed for where Luke Berringer would be waiting for him. Alex didn't turn to look back and see if Gayland had moved from his corner and towards the remaining tea and ice in the glass. He didn't need to. If he were a betting man, he would have bet that Gayland was standing by the remains of the iced tea, lamenting why he could not partake in the earthly pleasures that were denied to him.

He reached Luke Berringer's room and caught Jim outside the door, which was shut for the moment to keep private any conversation occurring outside of the room. "Thanks for coming over Alex. Luke returned from his appointment with Doctor Ruiz and seemed genuinely very happy and excited. I left him alone for a few minutes and when I went in to check on him, he was frantic and pacing around his room," Jim explained.

"Any idea what might have happened?" Alex quizzed Jim.

"None," Jim answered.

Alex gingerly pushed open Luke's door and spied him dialing the phone in his room in a frantic way. Luke caught the movement out of the corner of his eye and held out the receiver connected to an older looking landline phone, towards Alex. "I can't reach her! I have dialed several times and she won't pick up," Luke frantically bellowed!

"Maybe she is just unable to answer the phone, Luke. Who knows, she might be somewhere where she can't pick up. It happens to me and Courtney all the time," Alex responded.

Luke looked at Alex in a manner that said not this time, not this situation at all! "Stephanie told me to call her the second I got back to my room from my visit with the Doctor. She made me promise I would call her the second I got back. That was over an hour ago," Luke implored.

Alex tried calling Stephanie's phone number on his personal cell phone but just like with Luke's experience she didn't answer. Just as Alex hung up, his cell phone rang. The caller ID on his phone displayed *Glen Firestone.* Answering the phone, Alex heard a tone in Pastor Firestone's voice he couldn't recall ever hearing. "Alex, this is Glen Firestone. You alone?" He asked.

"No, I'm visiting with Luke Berringer, Stephanie's husband, right now."

"That's unfortunate. Can you get somewhere private to talk?" Glen questioned.

Excusing himself from Luke under the premise that he had a personal call, Alex stepped out of the room and down the hallway out of earshot of Luke. "Okay Pastor, I can talk privately now," Alex responded.

Glen Firestone paused for a moment before speaking. "Stephanie Berringer is dead! A car skipped the medium and hit several people waiting at the bus stop. She was the only person killed in the accident!"

Alex had no response. He stood numb in the hallway absorbing what Glen had just told him. "I'll need to call you later Glen," Alex spoke as he hung up the phone. He slid down the bright white cinder block wall until he had come to a sitting position on the polished linoleum floor.

Chapter 45:
Flashback

LUKE'S FATHER HELD HIS SON AROUND THE SHOULDERS as Glen Firestone spoke at the funeral for Stephanie Berringer. He did his best to hold his son and give him strength. He had seen his son struggle in this lifetime but never as much as at this moment. Alex and Courtney were seated two rows directly behind where Luke and his father sat. Alex watched and he saw that Luke's breathing was strained and intermittent between sobs of despair over the loss of his love, his reason for existing. Alex couldn't comprehend what Luke was feeling right now. He could only understand it as the anger he felt when Demetri threatened to approach Courtney while they were grieving over the supposed death of their child. Alex mourned for Luke and how this senseless act had stolen his new future away from him. Sitting next to Courtney was Cindy Firestone with her fiancé Tyler next to her. He looked down to see Courtney's hand in Cindy's and was grateful they were there for each other.

Glen had asked Alex to say some words at the gravesite based on his friendship with both Luke and Stephanie. He had struggled with what to say since public speaking wasn't Alex's forte, but the proper words were divinely inspired when Luke had demanded that Alex tell him why God had allowed this to happen? Alex knew he must address these questions not only for Luke's sake, but also for anybody else at the gravesite service that might have the same questions.

When everybody had settled into their spots at the gravesite and Glen Firestone had requested that Alex come forward to say a few words, Alex removed Courtney's arm from his and stood up to walk towards the side of the casket which held his friend. He cleared his throat the best he could wishing he had brought a bottle of water with him. He glanced over at Courtney who gave him that look of reassurance that said 'You got this'. Alex began to speak, and as he spoke, he became more confident that his words were representing God's thoughts. As Alex was nearing the end of his memorial for his friend Stephanie, he was interrupted in mid-sentence.

Not knowing if it was a flashback to a memory of his, or if it was real this time, Alex saw Gayland standing with two other demons just down the slight slope away from the casket. Just as soon as these images appeared before him, they were gone. The audience at the gravesite was perplexed by the long pause taken by Alex, but the content of his words had been accepted as uplifting so they seemed to acknowledge that he might have just forgotten his words for a moment.

He shook hands with the small gravesite party and after bidding farewell to Glen Firestone, Alex returned to sit down next to Courtney who had waited quietly and patiently for his part in Stephanie's funeral to be over. She immediately recognized that her husband seemed preoccupied in thought, but it disturbed her to see the look on his face as she studied him. 'What's the matter honey?" Courtney quizzed him.

There was a brief pause before he answered her with a slight tremble in his voice, "I had a flashback to my father's funeral," Alex responded. She acknowledged, sympathetically, how hard speaking at the gravesite memorial must have been for him. Alex stared out into the cemetery landscape as if he were disconnected to the events of the moment. "It wasn't the memory of my dad's funeral that bothered me."

"Then what?" Courtney implored.

Alex paused another moment then looked directly at his wife before answering. "I just realized where I've seen Gayland before."

Once they had returned home after Stephanie Berringer's funeral, Alex began to put together the pieces of his history involving Gayland sightings. At his father's funeral. At his home while sitting on the porch. In the Church parking lot standing in the rain. At the hospital, spying on him walking with Cindy Firestone. All of these were not coincidences. This demon had been stalking him like a shadow ever since he was a boy. Lurking in the mist like a predator animal. Gayland wasn't on a mission to gather souls for his master. He, Alex, was his mission. Putting two and two together, Alex realized Gayland was following him, gathering information to relay back to Lucifer. Demetri was a demon who just happened to have gotten in the way.

In a way, Alex felt he should be angry. He was angry, not at Gayland, but more so at himself. Angry that it took him so long to discover the truth. The truth was that Lucifer didn't really know *what* Alex was. It perplexed him and challenged his reign as Prince of an unbelieving world. Gayland was following his master's bidding, because the underworld was confused by this mortal who could travel and do the bidding of Gabriel's God, like an Angel.

Alex decided he had had enough of disguises and masquerades by his attending demons. It was time for them to fish or cut bait, to coin an old phrase used by many in the northwest fishing business.

Chapter 46:
The Farm

HE WALKED UP THE WOOD STAIRS and stepped onto his shaded porch in the front of his farmhouse. Looking out over what used to be barley fields, according to the mortal Alex, Gayland wondered why he had been summoned here. He pondered if Lucifer had required a meeting with him. These meetings with his master always brought him much anxiety. He shuddered to consider that a demon could have anxiety.

Gayland immediately noticed that there were two rocking chairs sitting facing each other. It had been a long time since two rocking chairs sat on this porch, and this felt very odd to him. Sitting next to *his* rocking chair, on the modest little table next to it, was a familiar glass of sweet tea with ice floating in a clear mason jar. What was different this time was the drips of condensation from the jar. He had never witnessed those drips before on sojourns to his farm.

The screen door at the front of the farmhouse was open and Gayland saw a shadow of a figure nearing the door from inside and opening it with a squeak brought on by years of neglect and lack of oil to its hinges. Emerging from the inside of the farmhouse appeared Alex Dante.

Gayland spoke to him immediately. Partly out of fear, but mostly from reverence. "Ah, it is you, Dante. It appears you have visited my sanctuary before. This explains your knowledge of its history."

Alex, who was not in the mood for small talk with the demon, pointed at the pair of rockers sitting on the front porch that were badly in need of paint. "Sit, Gayland. We have much to discuss, much to decide," stated Alex.

Remembering the recent impatience, he had witnessed from Alex, Gayland was compelled to immediately comply. "As you wish, mor…, uhm Alex." Sitting down in his accustomed chair, Gayland could not take his eyes off the jar with the tea surrounding fresh ice cubes.

Alex could see the longing look in Gayland's demon eyes.

"It's one of your earthly desires, isn't it?" Alex questioned knowing fully the answer.

"Perhaps. The liquid intrigues me, but alas, it is only a fancy of your mortal world. As an angel of Lucifer, I am not permitted to enjoy earthly pleasures, let alone partake," Gayland answered.

"Says who?" Alex responded to elicit thought from his demon companion.

"Well, my master, of course. To partake of earthly pleasures would make them my idol. I am beholden to my god, and he only," Gayland answered with a continued focus on the tea.

"What would happen if you were to partake?" Alex quizzed.

"I'm not sure. I would probably experience no pleasure, no sensation and my master would remove me from this place forever," Gayland replied.

"If he could remove you from this place, then explain how it is that *I* have brought you here. How did I know about your farm, your earthly desires?" Alex quipped in a rather arrogant manner.

Gayland was forced to consider his answer despite wanting to respond with all the arrogance of his demon intellect. "I suppose that's the answer we all seek don't we, Alex Dante. Even my master."

Alex sat back in the rocking chair he had provided for himself and, with one leg crossed over the other, began to rock. For what seemed like an eternity to Gayland, and being immortal, he knew of eternities very well, Alex simply rocked while looking out over the landscape. Eventually he turned his head towards Gayland and replied in a calm manner. "Your master desires to be here right now. He's disturbed that I'm here with you."

"How do you know this, mortal?" Gayland replied with some indignation.

"Because I have bound him from this place!" Alex answered.

Mesmerized by what Alex had just said to him, Gayland was even more entranced by his next statement. "I can tell you why I have dominion over your sanctuary Gayland. I can end your years of struggling to get those answers about me. I can ensure that you can remain on this farm, your sanctuary, maybe not for an eternity but you will know peace for many earthly years."

"Please tell me how you can do this?" Gayland insisted with his curiosity peaked.

"Just take a drink of that tea. Once you have drunk it, felt the cold of the liquid on your demon tongue, tasted the sweetness, you'll have the truth and my protection from your master so that he can no longer control you or sentence you. This will be your and my covenant."

"And what if I determine you are deceiving me, mortal?"

"Then you'll never know the answer to the question. You've got nothing to lose and only what I now show you to gain," Alex pointed to an open root cellar which was adjacent to the old farmhouse. Inside the root cellar a portal opened, and Gayland heard the cries and anguish of lost souls emitting from it.

"You have this power? Am I to believe you have this power?" Gayland asked as he gazed at the portal.

"Is Lucifer here to challenge me?" Alex quipped.

"So, you know it was me who followed you all these years? You know what I was seeking?"

"Drink the tea, Gayland. Then you'll know those answers. I don't lie and deceive, demon. That is your bag."

Gayland could not take his eyes off the jar of iced tea. As his demon hand moved ever so slowly towards the jar, Alex could see a slight tremble in his demon hand. He grasped the jar in his hand and for a moment, Gayland felt the cool drips of water on his demon hand.

"Please, tell me what that is that I feel on my physical hand?" Gayland asked with a sense of how a child might ask.

"Condensation, Gayland. It's condensation that forms on a hard surface when the liquid inside is colder than the air outside the jar. It's a slight example of the human pleasure you'll feel if you bring the jar to your lips and drink."

Just the pleasure he had derived from the water drops on his demon hand was almost enough to tempt Gayland to bring the jar towards his demon mouth and face eternal pain if Alex was lying to him.

Alex watched as Gayland contemplated whether it was worth it, to risk everything he knew as a demon of Lucifer, to have a few years before the rapture and the Glorious second coming of Jesus Christ. To know as much peace as a demon could experience. He knew Gayland would never have eternal life, his name would never be written in the Book of Life, but he could capture some earthly pleasures.

"I won't force you to make your decision with me here at your sanctuary. I will leave this place while you decide. The same decision I had to make to follow Christ or your master, I offer you the opportunity to live without fear of retribution from your master," Alex offered.

With those words spoken by Alex, Gayland was left holding the jar with his hand still trembling. Alex was gone.

Chapter 47:
Uplift

COURTNEY WAS ANXIOUS FOR ALEX TO ARRIVE HOME. She knew the challenge he faced in using Gayland as a tool to bring around the eventual meeting he would have with Satan. She also knew her husband was strong in the Lord, but she still worried about him knowing he would face the true deceiver of the world. Satan was cunning and ancient; her loving husband was an attendant in a mental hospital who had been anointed by God. She was anxious to hear about his supernatural adventure and to have him feel the first kicks of his baby.

As if those events weren't enough to bring on anxiety from her, Pastor Firestone had called. He seemed a bit frantic but didn't want to share with her why he needed to talk directly to Alex. When Alex walked through the door, she threw her arms around his neck and hugged him like never before.

"I'm fine, love. Sorry to have worried you. Perhaps it would be better to not let you know about my escapades," Alex said with all sincerity.

"No! You must never shut me out! I just worry about you, but I know God's got your back. I want you to tell me how everything went down with Gayland, but before you do, you must call Pastor Firestone. He was very adamant about speaking with you as soon as you got home."

"Hmmm, I wonder what's going on?" Alex replied as he dialed Glen Firestone's phone number. Glen answered his phone and was relieved that the call was from Alex.

"Thank God it's you Alex!

"What's up Pastor? Courtney said you were frantic to speak with me."

"Yes, I'm on my way to Luke Berringer's father's house. He called me because Luke's drunk and out of control. He doesn't want to call the police, but he doesn't know what to do."

"I'm on my way. Give me his address and I'll meet you there."

He could see the look of disappointment in Courtney's eyes. She had heard the conversation between Alex and Glen. "Go! You must go!" Courtney insisted. "I love you," Alex called to his wife as he grabbed his coat and went back out the door.

When Alex arrived, Glen Firestone was already at the house. He jogged to the front door and was met by Luke's father. "Pastor Firestone's in the back bedroom, it's on the right. He's with Luke. He's in bad shape Alex!"

Alex just nodded and moved swiftly through the house and down the hallway to the bedroom. When he arrived at the bedroom door, he found Glen Firestone sitting on the floor next to Luke who was sobbing uncontrollably. Luke looked up at Alex with bloodshot eyes. The type of eyes a man, or woman, has when they've given up.

Alex could tell by the smell that alcohol had once again gained control of his friend. Luke's father arrived in the doorway. "I'm so sorry to have bothered you and Glen. I just didn't know what else to do. He just hasn't been the same since Stephanie died. I'm so worried they'll arrest him again!"

Alex turned and met Luke's father at the doorway. He placed his arm around him in a reassuring way and said, "You did the right thing. Right now, your son needs us, but he needs God even more, he just doesn't realize it right now."

He patted Luke's father on the back and returned his attention to Luke and Glen who were still sitting on the floor leaning upright against the bed. Alex went to the opposite side of Luke from where Glen was sitting. Both sober men looked at each other and immediately knew, the best thing they could do at this moment for a fallen brother was to just pray and be there.

As the vigil continued and night passed into the early hours of the morning, Glen and Alex came to a time when sleep finally took their troubled friend. They acknowledged this with each other and, with Alex lifting Luke up by the shoulders and Glen lifting the legs, they were able to bring Luke off the floor and into the bed next to him. The men, realizing they had a moment to relax from the efforts of consoling Luke, stepped out into the living room. Luke's father had also slipped into slumber in his recliner, so the men stepped out onto the front porch to talk.

"What now Alex?" Glen questioned.

Alex replied, "I can't blame him, Pastor. He honestly believes God has let him down. I know, and you know, that isn't true, but Luke doesn't know that."

"Did you see a demon with him?" Glen asked with reluctance afraid of the answer.

"Not tonight. This isn't the work of a demon. This is the work of sin and Satan himself. I apologize Pastor for not letting you know this earlier, Luke had the same demon before his rebirth as Cindy," Alex answered in a repentant tone.

Glen stared at the ground upon hearing these words spoken by Alex. Then raising his head and eyes to look directly into Alex's he spoke in a manner Alex had not heard before. "Is it wrong for me to want this demon gone from this world? Is it wrong for me to desire for him to be destroyed? Can you destroy this vile, hateful creature, Alex?"

Alex answered his Pastor as earnestly as he could, "I thought Gabriel had done it for me, Pastor. I believed he was gone from inflicting his torment on any other mortal. I was wrong." Alex sighed and continued, "I was wrong to have underestimated Satan all this time, when we know he is truly behind this evil. The demon that possessed your daughter and Luke is being manipulated by an even more powerful demon, and the source of *all* evil, Satan. Now that I have learned, by the grace of God, what my job here on earth is, and will be, I will answer your question. All we need to do is look to the word. The word says that not even Satan, let alone a demon, can physically harm a human. But just as the evil one cannot *destroy* a mortal; I cannot *destroy* a demon. Please take ease in his word. The evil one and his host will be cast away by our Lord."

Glen Firestone grabbed Alex's hands and the two men prayed together.

"Pastor, we'll need to get Luke into a full-time residential rehab facility. One that will bring the word of God to his heart. Only through the grace of God and the word, can Luke be healed," Alex spoke with truth and assurance.

Glen answered, "I'll get a group at the Church together and we'll find that place for him. Until then, we'll be with him twenty-four, seven."

"Great, Pastor. I'm blessed to have you as a friend," Alex replied.

"No, I think it is *I* that am blessed to have *you* as a friend," Glen responded.

Alex could see the faint rays of the morning sun beginning to poke their light above the horizon. He smiled at Glen Firestone and said, "I might not be able to destroy a fallen angel Pastor, but God has certainly anointed me to put them in their place. I must take my leave of you and go about that duty right now."

Glen was about to say go with God, thinking that Alex would leave to go jump in his car, but before he could get the words from his mouth, Alex was instantly gone from his sight.

Chapter 48:
Exposed

DEMETRI WAS STARTLED TO BE STANDING in the front of an old farmhouse. There was dirt and weeds surrounding his feet. The tranquility of the lake had been snatched away from him, and now he had been transported to this old and dirty structure with white peeling paint over wood siding. His demon equilibrium returned to him, and he spied Gayland sitting on the porch of the decaying structure, holding something in his hand and trembling.

"Is this your sanctuary Gayland? If so, why have I been brought to this despicable, dirty place to be in your presence?" Demetri asked of his old nemesis.

Gayland had no answer for his recently arrived guest. In fact, Demetri's presence only helped to exacerbate the dilemma that faced Gayland.

"My apologies if I've offended you, Gayland. I just expected more of you if this is your place of refuge," Demetri said in a smug and demeaning manner.

"Spare me your indignation, Demetri. I expect you came to this place the same way I did. No matter what you might think of my solitude here, I have my reasons for being here. I'm sure your sanctuary might seem repugnant to me also," Gayland retorted.

Demetri shook his demon head in reaffirmation of Gayland's retort. "Yes, so I have been told." Demetri looked about the acreage and returned to his conversation with his fellow fallen spirit. "Then I assume I was summoned here by the mortal."

"Yes, I believe you were, just as I was," Gayland confirmed Demetri's suspicion.

Gayland placed the mason jar of cold iced tea back onto the small table next to his chair. In doing so he felt somewhat relieved from the pressure of wanting to take Alex up on his offer to live out the next several years free from control by anybody. Still, by putting down the jar, he also lost the sensation of 'cool' and 'wet' from the condensation. He already desperately missed it. He felt a yearning that was foreign to him. Still, the sensations would not leave his demon thoughts. Demetri's focus went directly to the jar of tea. "What's that by your side Gayland?" Demetri quizzed him.

"None of your business. Why don't you leave me," Gayland called out to the figure standing before him at the front of the porch.

"I have no desire to be here. If I had my druthers I would've never come here. If the mortal, Alex Dante, has indeed brought both of us here, it can be for no good, considering whom our master is."

Gayland laughed at Demetri's comment. "You have no idea, Demetri. You have no idea just how special this place is to me. Why I choose it as my sanctuary. Why I find my peace here."

Demetri had to grant him that statement. He had his special place too. His lake held those demon memories and proximity to two of the most precious and haunting hosts he had ever had. The girl with the alabaster eyes and Annabel.

Then Gayland answered Demetri's glaring question. "This is what the humans call 'iced tea'. The elements floating inside the brown liquid are frozen water. Water that is frozen is cold, unlike anything we have felt before. The liquid is cold from the ice, and it is sweet as it enters your throat, and it brings a quenching to your thirst."

"And why tell me this Gayland? It is not for us to know or *feel* these things!" Demetri retorted.

"Ah, but perhaps it is."

"How?" Demetri asked.

"The mortal has offered this to me. He has offered this to me and to live out my days here with nobody to fear, including our master."

"The mortal does not have this power," Demetri quipped in hope it would be accepted by Gayland as the truth.

"I believe he just might," answered Gayland.

"You aren't seriously considering this?" Demetri asked.

With that question Gayland reached for the jar and took it once again into his hand. Demetri, enraged by this action, jumped forward onto the porch where Gayland sat and slapped the jar from his hand. As it fell to the porch, the glass shattered, spilling the liquid contents.

"**You lazy traitor!**" Demetri called out with the anger of a pro wrestler before a cage match! "Our master will be here any moment for you!"

Gayland, who now stood, pushed Demetri away from him and pointed towards the floor of the porch where the liquid had spilled, and the jar had been broken. "If I am so wrong and a traitor to *your* beloved master, then why has this occurred?" Gayland watched as Demetri's angered look became one of disbelief and astonishment. Sitting on the table, next to Gayland's chair was an intact, full mason jar bespeckled with drops of condensation and containing the finest iced tea ever brewed interspersed with several ice cubes.

Chapter 49:
Sanctuary

JIM JOHNSON WAS A FOURTH-GENERATION FARMER. His family had homesteaded this land and worked it with their sweat and blood long before Oregon became a state in the Union. Farmland in the upper section of eastern Oregon was rich and fertile and the Johnson property was prized land for just how fertile it was.

For a farmer to find and take a wife was often difficult in these parts. For sons and daughters of these farmers long hours devoted to the farm was the norm. The only way for one of the children of the farm to meet a potential spouse was at the occasional barn raising or church social.

That is exactly how Jim met Sarah. Jim was the only child of his parents, and at the age of twenty-seven had taken over the family farm due to his parents' death from measles. For a young man of twenty-seven to take over running a farm the size of the Johnson's wasn't unusual. Farming was hard, and if sickness didn't take you at a young age, hard work did!

Jim and Sarah met at the local church and were immediately drawn to each other. Jim never felt close to God, nor did he ever read his bible. Truth be known the only reason he attended church was so he could meet with and court his beloved Sarah. She was seventeen when she and Jim were married, and they both worked the farm with the same drive and love for the land. They were a match made in heaven.

Despite the land and soil being fertile, Sarah wasn't. It weighed heavy on their minds that they would have no children to inherit the farm, but they both worked it just as hard. So hard, that at the age of forty, Sarah came down with pneumonia and died.

The match made in heaven, now received the cursing of Jim Johnson. Without the love of his life by his side and an heir to inherit his land, Jim spent the rest of his days cursing God, although he had never really believed in him.

This was when Gayland came to Jim. He was ripe for the taking and Gayland knew that based on this mortal's indulgence in homemade moonshine, it wouldn't be long before he drank himself into the deliverance of his soul for Gayland to present to his master.

Jim became a recluse. Moonshine made him an unpleasant person to be around so as time went by few people came to visit Jim. His reputation as a drunk, and slightly off in the head, resulted in those few people that normally visited him, eventually disappearing. What came to pass is, nobody came to see Jim anymore.

Every now and then, Jim would quit drinking and clean himself up along with his ever-dilapidating farmhouse. He would take a large jar and place wrapped tea bags into the jar. He would walk out to the well near the front porch and pump water into the jar until the bags were suspended and beginning to leak saturated tea into the water.

Gayland was mesmerized by this action. Jim would set the jar out in the sunshine for several hours and return to his rocking chair on the porch and just rock back and forth in that same chair for hours. He would watch as Jim slapped his hands on his pants, rose and fetched the tea from the step which it was resting upon while brewing.

Taking the jar with the brown liquid into his kitchen, Jim poured fresh honey from the beehives he kept on the farm into the liquid. He would stir the liquid and walk to the cupboard and grab two mason jars. He would then walk to his meager ice box, crack the metal ice tray in the freezer releasing the ice, and place the ice into the jars.

Ice was fascinating to Gayland. He could only imagine how delightful this mortal invention could be. He would watch Jim pour the liquid over the ice until the jars were filled. Then what happened next made Gayland even more intrigued. His human, Jim, who was intoxicated nearly all the time would carry the mason jars with the iced tea out onto the porch, pull up a second rocking chair and sit and rock, while drinking his tea, and having a three-hour conversation with his beloved Sarah, who was not there.

He witnessed this event several times over the course of his time with Jim. Gayland wondered why he would drink only tea, talk to his dead wife for several hours, put away the iced tea and jars and return to his moonshine jug until he was no longer coherent about the world around him. What perplexed Gayland the most is that he had nothing to do with this behavior, Jim accomplished this all on his own.

One day, at the end of Jim's earthly existence, he sat drinking iced tea and conversing with his Sarah on the porch. Gayland stood at the front of the porch with his demon rear end resting on the porch railing. Jim looked up at him. He looked directly at Gayland who tried to figure out what he was looking at. Then he spoke directly to Gayland, "I've spoken with my wife. Even though she is with God now, she and I have decided to give you the farm, Gayland." With those words, Jim's head and upper body slumped and he was dead.

Gayland never revealed this to his master. He could not reveal that Alex was not the first mortal to see and speak to him. In fact, there had been many. As he watched the portal open, and Jim's soul walk to the opening, he wondered for a moment why Jim had never turned to Gabriel's God? He could have rejoined his beloved again in *that* paradise. Even if he might have wanted to, now it was too late. His master had claimed his soul.

Chapter 50:
Decisions

THE MASON JAR THAT HAD MAGICALLY REAPPEARED with iced tea was once again in Gayland's hand. He glanced at Demetri who seemed incapable of challenging him this time.

"Whatever makes you desire to drink this earthly concoction will only fail you. I have never been an advocate for you Gayland, but this time I must tell you that you are deceived," Demetri pleaded.

Gayland brought the jar to his demon lips, smiled at Demetri, and began to feel the cold sweet nectar of truth cascade down his demon throat. Demetri watched as his fellow demon drank the mortal fluid, wondering how he could get back to his lake to see if he could summon his master and tell him of the deceit he had witnessed at the hands of Gayland. Perhaps then he would be restored to honor. Just as soon as that thought entered Demetri's head, he was back standing on his boat dock with the light above him beginning to flicker to signal the impending darkness.

Gayland looked out from his porch over the farm. He looked over at Alex who had only just appeared in the last few moments after Demetri's departure. "You have received the truth, Gayland," Alex said.

"Yes, as you promised. I will still be banished from this earth when that time comes. I know now that I won't have this place forever, and I will eventually become a captive of the portal. But until that time, when I must confess that Jesus is Lord, I can remain at peace here."

"As promised," Alex affirmed.

Gayland understood he would eventually face an eternity of torture and pain, but until then he would exist in peace, here at his sanctuary, until he would see the true God gather them all to be chained together at a different lake. One lake that Demetri would not find pleasant. This made him smile an even broader demon smile.

His memories reverted to Farmer Johnson and Andrea Best. Two mortals that had the same ability to see and talk with demons just as Alex Dante could. He was glad he never exposed their ability to his master, although Lucifer probably learned this fact from the farmer's soul. Gayland realized now that Lucifer had deceived them all. He began to rock, sipping his iced tea, just like Gabriel, as he watched Alex vanish.

Chapter 51:
Confrontation

LUCIFER PACED UP AND DOWN THE BOAT DOCK. Demetri was in fear that his master was beyond angry at what had been revealed about his recent meeting with Gayland. It took several minutes for Lucifer to speak. "Excellent job my dear Demetri. Excellent job!"

Demetri was surprised by Lucifer's praise. He wondered if it was said in sarcasm, and he bowed his head a little deeper into his demon chest in hopes of diverting any wrath that might be directed towards him.

"Tell me, my Demetri, prior to me bringing you back here, did Gayland speak of the mortal Alex Dante and how he gained the power to see us and know of our existence?" Lucifer quizzed in an attempt to be nonchalant.

"No, my lord, he did not. As I relayed to you, he said once he tasted of the liquid that held the lies of the mortal, he would know from where the mortal's powers derived," Demetri responded as Lucifer pondered his answer.

"Yes, perhaps I should have kept you there a little longer," Lucifer lied despite knowing full well he no longer had any power to gain audience with Gayland. A third voice entered the conversation emulating from the pathway that led to the entrance of the dock. "Perhaps you should just bounce over there right now, Satan," Alex spoke with all the sarcasm he could summon.

Lucifer turned to see Alex standing there. Demetri brought up his head at the sound of Alex's voice. He knew that nothing good was going to come out of this meeting.

"Alex Dante, what a pleasure to have you in my audience," Satan hissed like the serpent he was. Satan, who was used to being in control of meetings with his servants, tried to recover at the sudden appearance of Alex Dante. It was obvious to Demetri that the mortal's presence had made his master uncomfortable. He tried to pass off Lucifer's defensive posture with the understanding that it had been over two thousand years since his master had a direct audience with a living mortal.

Lucifer, who always seemed in control of every situation thought to himself, 'Here he is. The human that has perplexed me for so long, standing before me. Giving commands to me! This earthly realm is mine, not his. I must see just how powerful his God has made him!' "So, my mysterious mortal. You travel as though you are spirit, just like my legion and the worshippers of Gabriel's God. But just as we do, you must manifest yourself to us in human form."

Alex calmly replied. "I owe you no explanation, Satan. My abilities are granted and provided to me by God. Soon enough, you will know this also."

Demetri stood motionless. He was mesmerized by the interchange happening between his master and his foe. In a way, he envied Alex Dante.

"Well then, if you prefer not to be courteous and respectful of me and my honored angel, then I must ask you to leave us since you were not invited," Satan lashed out, having lost patience with this impertinent human. Lucifer knew that none of what he bellowed was true. He had not come here on his own attrition, nor had he brought Demetri to this sanctuary. His arrival at Demetri's pathway had not been on his command. He must divert that knowledge away from Demetri or face humiliation before him.

Alex's rebuttal was Lucifer's worst fear. "Ah, but it was *I* that called you and your demon to this place!"

Demetri could see the anger beginning to swell in the mannerisms of Lucifer. Sensing this, Demetri felt it prudent to come to the aide of his master despite fearing that what Alex had just said, was true. Moving past Lucifer and towards Alex to place himself between them, Demetri pointed his demon finger at Alex and called out. "Do not disrespect my master with your lies. Nobody summons my master! Especially not a mortal like yourself."

Undaunted by the threatening nature being displayed by the demon Demetri, Alex held his ground, knowing this demon had no physical dominion over him. "Don't flatter yourself Demetri. Your master knows as well as you should, you have no power over me."

Satan realized that he was quickly losing this battle and must somehow flip the event. "**Demetri, stand down!** I don't need you to defend me! Let us be the more hospitable creatures here tonight."

Alex smirked on the inside knowing what was coming next.

"Mr. Dante, please tell us why you have called us here tonight? Is it to relish in the conquest over my faithful servant, Gayland, as Demetri has told me? Perhaps you could summon Gayland to us here, now, so I can wish him my best?" Satan said, knowing that it was a futile request.

Alex did not answer.

Demetri secretly wished he was in Gayland's position right now. His failures had clouded his demon conscious, and he spoke out in frustration. "Perhaps you should show reverence, mortal. A little respect towards this god before you could go a long way in seeing your child again. Your whore has already petitioned my master for this favor,"

Demetri sounded like a hiker in a cavern waiting for the echo to return.

Alex had to wear every scrap of God's armor after hearing those words from Demetri. "Demetri, you are a foul and vile being! I hope you understand I could vanquish you just as easily as Gabriel did before me!"

"Then why don't you?" Demetri questioned secretly hoping Alex would.

Lucifer intervened with a reconciled response. "I do not delight in any of this conversation. I am the god of this realm and wish you to release us. Go away, mortal, and leave us be."

"Yes, as my master has called out your lies, leave us and return to your mortal existence," Demetri requisitioned as a younger brother standing with the protection of his big brother.

Just as Alex was considering his next move with his demonic audience, a fourth voice called out from the night mist. "Demetri, the lies you have heard here come from the one you have placed your faith in all these years. Your angers and frustrations are from believing that my words are true."

That voice brought immediate recognition to Demetri. That voice that had haunted him these many years had returned. Demetri strained to see into the mist in hopes that a figure would appear. A figure that, if he were to see her again, would make all of this make sense. He understood why Gayland would do what he did. He would drink the liquid also if he could be with her again without interference.

He knew that voice and it belonged to none other than Annabel.

Chapter 52:
The Parlor

WORRIED ABOUT HER HUSBAND, Courtney prayed for his safety. She had not heard a word about Luke Berringer, and it was unlike Alex not to answer his cellphone or at least drop her a text that he was fine or busy.

"Lord, it is hard being the wife of God's servant. Please keep him safe. I need him too. I pray that he can let me know he is okay. These things I pray in your precious name, amen." Feeling the burden of fatigue from lack of sleep and worry, Courtney could no longer fight off sleep. As she slept, Courtney dreamed.

She was sitting on an antique sofa. Her palm and fingers moved across a velvet covering with tufted buttons that brought texture as rich as the color it was. A deep red, almost maroon if you wanted to call it. A young female child, perhaps three, maybe four, played with dolls at her feet. The child was beautiful. Golden hair with pigtails tied with floral bows.

Courtney felt a warm glow immolating deep within herself. The glow was happiness and peace. She looked out the window at the rays of sunshine as they created beams coming into the room where she sat and watched the child play. She looked up as a beautiful young woman came into the room carrying a silver tray with a floral porcelain teapot and four small cups to match. Courtney immediately recognized the beautiful woman as Annabel.

"Sorry, Courtney, this is how I envisioned perfection. A young mother, watching her daughter play in the parlor and preparing for early afternoon tea. I realize this is a vision from my era, not yours."

Courtney smiled and answered. "This is a delightful vision, dear Annabel. I so wish I could have seen your era."

"Well, this vision is a fantasy to me. It certainly was not my life." Annabel responded.

"I'm sorry, Annabel, Courtney replied.

"Oh, you needn't be sorry. My sanctuary in heaven is way beyond this. I can't wait for you to see," Annabel answered.

"Will it be soon?"

"Yes, very soon, and when you least expect it. Until that day, when our Lord comes to claim you, and your fellow believers from the earth, I have come to bring comfort to you, and news of Alex," Annabel tenderly said.

Excited for news about her husband, Courtney waited with eagerness for Annabel to share what she knew. "Alex has brought Lucifer to him. He is with him now. The demon Demetri is there also, but don't be afraid for Alex. I am there with him as is the entire host of God! As I said to you in your previous dream, my presence will be to assist and support Alex. I will accomplish that by turning the demon against his master. The demon Demetri will understand that the one he has worshiped for so long is the great deceiver." Hearing that her husband was well, and well protected, gave great comfort to Courtney.

"Alex will deliver the message to the serpent that the abyssal, the pathway to the underworld and the lake of fire, will be his upon the return of Jesus and his believers to earth after seven years. He is letting Satan know that for a thousand years he will be his jailer. The keeper of the portal. Satan will attempt to resist to accept this truth, but he will know that he, Satan, has no dominion over Alex." Annabel poured a cup of tea for Courtney and handed it to her. "Your husband will then be able to rest for a time and welcome the birth of his child into the world."

Courtney gazed into the beautiful ghostly eyes of her comforter and asked, "This child playing before me, is she your fantasy?"

"No, she is your reality," Annabel answered.

Chapter 53:
Truth

DEMETRI STARTED TO SEE THE VISION of Annabel manifesting herself in physical form. He strained to see her as the mist slightly distorted her features. With every passing moment the image of Annabel became ever clearer to him. He thrilled at this encounter. This is the only soul that he never wanted to release. If he had a mortal heart, it would be beating very fast.

All perception of Alex and his master disappeared. Demetri's sole focus and attention was on Annabel. He struggled to find his voice to speak to her. He knew he must. To miss this opportunity to let her know he was sorry for leaving her would pale in comparison to an eternity of torment. "For so long I have yearned to be with you again. You knew me for only a moment, but I knew you, Annabel, for much longer," Demetri bared his demon soul, knowing that it also made him vulnerable.

He noticed Lucifer seemed upset at the appearance of Annabel. His expression perplexed Demetri because it could have only been his master that allowed her to be present. Certainly the mortal Alex, could not have known about her or have the power to summon her? Alex's power could not extend to souls that belonged to his master. The

189

internal conflict Demetri was experiencing caused him to be on heightened alert.

Annabel addressed Demetri in a firm but patient manner. "You left me too soon, demon."

To call him a *demon* pained Demetri. He was an angel and she, having been mortal once, should pay him that respect. He glanced back at Lucifer to see if he, too, was upset at her lack of respect and even more so, her presence here. This was uncharted territory for him conversing with a delivered soul.

"You were a coward Demetri. You could not stay until the end because you were a coward! Because of that glorious error on your part, I was redeemed. Not by the evil one, but by my Lord and savior, Jesus Christ."

Those words spoken by Annabel brought a piercing shriek to Demetri's demon ears. It was like an air raid siren blasting within close distance. "You appear here, before me, at the grace of *our* master. I delivered your soul to *him*," Demetri demanded.

Alex had not inserted himself into the interchange between Demetri and Annabel. He had no need. Annabel was accomplishing exactly what the Lord wished her to do. He also took no pleasure in their conversation. It pained him to witness even a demon being deceived by Lucifer. Demetri looked at Annabel in disbelief and then turned his pleading gaze on Lucifer. "Please master, god of this earth, my lord, silence this mortal ghost. I cannot bear this blasphemy."

Having no power over Annabel, Lucifer could not respond to Demetri's request.

Defeated, Demetri resigned himself to his master's silence. He bowed his head in a painful posture and spoke, "I was deceived in heaven, and now I have been deceived here on earth. I have no power here. I have no power to resist the authority of Alex Dante, I have no power to withstand Gabriel, and now the only cherished memory I have of this mortal woman, has been destroyed."

Alex stepped forward and with several of the heavenly host appearing behind him, including Gabriel, proclaimed to his demon audience of Satan and Demetri, "Be it known that Jesus Christ is Lord. I witness his coming in the clouds to claim his believers from this earth. You, Demetri, are one of the fallen, along with this one you call *master.* You will have your moment here on earth until the day of the Lord coming. When that day comes, you will bow your knee and your tongue will profess that Jesus Christ is Lord."

"And what of you, mortal? What will become of you from this day forward?" Satan hissed in defeat.

"You will see me again. After your time on this earth is finished, you will see me for a thousand years! As the keeper of your prison."

Demetri could no longer see Annabel. She was gone as before except, this time, he would no longer carry her memory with him. The pathway to the underworld opened and Alex permitted Satan and Demetri to enter. Should Demetri ever return to this earth it would be up to Satan to make it so. He was a demon and very soon they would have a different perspective on the mortals of this earth. Alex knew one thing by the grace of God, and that was that until the rapture, he might never see an Angel or demon again.

Just before Demetri disappeared into the portal, Alex called out to him one last time. "Demon Demetri, you won't find my child where you go now. By the grace of my God, she lives, and she will watch you in bondage as she plays above you." He honestly didn't intend to rub salt into the wound of a defeated demon. Well, maybe he did, just a little.

Chapter 54:
Joined

CINDY FIRESTONE-MCINTYRE WALKED OVER to her bridesmaid and carefully gave her a big hug. "Thank you for delaying the birth of your baby girl so I could nail down this handsome fellow who works for my father," Cindy laughed.

Courtney was still perplexed at how she had managed to make her bridesmaids dress fit over her ever expanding mid-section. Alex came over to join the two favorite women in his life. Cindy was able to give them both a joint hug. "I'm so glad to have you both here to celebrate with Tyler and me. I was just telling Courtney that she has my permission to steal the show at any time to have this kid."

Luke Berringer also approached the group to offer his congratulations. Alex was pleased that he was well enough to attend and praised him about how good he looked. He also knew that Luke had a long way to go, but at least the demons he now faced in his life would not be real.

It had been a long time since Alex had visited with Martha Firestone who had just arrived to join the immediate party. Martha could not resist touching Courtney's belly, but Courtney had become used to it by now. In fact, she had almost come to expect it.

"It's a girl, right?" Martha quizzed.

"Yes, it's a girl, Courtney answered.

"Have you picked out a name yet?" Martha asked in a normal motherly fashion.

Alex and Courtney looked at each other with broad smiles on their faces as Courtney answered, "Annabel. We're going to name her Annabel."

Chapter 55:
Celebration

ALEX ALMOST WISHED that there was a demon to witness to right now because his ability to move like an Angel in his mortal world was not provided to him unless it involved one of Lucifer's legions. "This stupid traffic. I don't ever remember seeing this much traffic in Astoria in my life. Of course, until now," he cried out in exasperation.

"It will be fine Dad," Courtney softly spoke just before wincing in pain from another contraction. She grabbed the handle above the passenger door with her right hand in order to hoist herself into a more comfortable position. Her reassurance to Alex did not make him feel any better. He wondered if every father struggled like this right before his first child was to be born. "I think it was easier to face Satan himself than to go through this," Alex confided to his wife who sat next to him in the car breathing in rhythm to ease the contraction pains.

"Alex, it's two thirty in the morning. There's only been one other car on the road, and we passed it ten minutes ago," Courtney reminded her exasperated husband.

He responded, "Well, one too many for me!"

Both father and mother-to-be couldn't help but laugh despite Courtney once again wincing in pain. Six hours later, a tired couple held and dedicated a little baby girl to Jesus. Annabel Dante had jet black hair, just like her father.

Chapter 56:
Rage of Ages

LUCIFER SAT ALONE. His rage over what transpired at the lake had at last dispersed. He had banished Demetri from his presence. He wasn't sure if he would, or could, ever use the demon again. In the endgame, it wasn't Demetri that had failed. It was him. He wasn't going to accept the fate that was outlined for him. This human might have been anointed with powers from heaven, but he was far to cunning of a god to allow this mortal to dictate his future to him.

"I require loyalty. I am benevolent, and just, to my servants who are loyal," He reassured himself. It was then that the thunder and fire swirled about him as his anger returned. Once again, he calmed himself and channeled his focus on commanding the true object of his rage and despise to appear before him at his throne. His powers failed him. His Kingdom must not be denied, and revenge now constituted his very existence and thought.

Satan rose from his throne and summoned his closest legion of demons. Among them was Orin, a vile, but resourceful creature. With the use of his very thoughts, he commissioned Orin to seek, and find, the *one* demon who stood in the way of his triumph as god of the Earth.

In total obedience Orin took command of the earthly legion of demons, and with a bow of reverence for his master, he traveled up the portal to find and capture the demon, Gayland.